Brolin

The gunfighter known as Brolin was thought to have been dead for the past ten years. That was until Red Mike Stall and his outlaws hijacked the westbound train and attempted to murder everyone on board. Stall recognized Brolin from the old days and left him to burn in the abandoned church with the other passengers.

He should have shot Brolin then and there because the gunfighter managed to escape and now is dogging the bloody trail Stall has left in his wake.

With the help of Emmett King, a greenhorn store owner who lost his son to a stray bullet from the outlaws, the pair eventually catch up to Stall in the town of Miller's Crossing.

In a final bloody showdown, can a dead man win the day? Or will a killer continue his murderous rampage across the high country?

And what is the secret Brolin is hiding?

By the same author

Fury at Bent Fork

Brolin

B. S. Dunn

ROBERT HALE

First published in Great Britain 2016

ISBN 978-0-7198-2098-4

The Crowood Press
The Stable Block
Crowood Lane
Ramsbury
Marlborough
Wiltshire SN8 2HR

www.bhwesterns.com

Robert Hale is an imprint
of The Crowood Press

Typeset by
Derek Doyle & Associates, Shaw Heath
Printed and bound in Great Britain by
CPI Group (UK) Ltd, Croydon, CR0 4YY

This one is for Sam and Jacob.

PROLOGUE

Ellsworth Trail, 1875

Brolin shifted in the saddle and the leather creaked. Something about this job made him feel uneasy.

Out on the grassy plain, amid the moonlit darkness, a coyote yipped. Brolin's horse shifted nervously. Cows lowed, protesting against the animal's presence.

He patted the horse gently on its muscular neck. 'Easy boy,' he whispered.

'The men are ready, Brolin,' Mike Stall told the gunfighter in a low voice. 'Just say the word and we'll hit the herd and start it runnin'.'

Brolin nodded. 'Just remember, when they take off, turn 'em away from the camp. Morgan said he just wanted 'em scattered so he could arrive at Ellsworth first and get top price. He don't want anyone gettin' killed.'

Morgan had hired Brolin to oversee the cattle drive he was making to Ellsworth. Even though he was a gun for hire, Brolin was a damn good ramrod. He'd made the trip three times over the past four years and his herds had made it through every time with minimal loss. And they always arrived at the railhead first.

This year he was working for Cyrus Morgan's Circle M and the drive had been troubled from the start. They'd set out with 2,000 head of longhorns and a fifteen-man crew.

After just two days on the trail they lost their first man. He was gored in the leg, which severed his femoral artery, and he died from blood loss soon after. The second man drowned in the Red River crossing and a further two were lost to outlaws in the Nations.

The scattering of the herd and the ensuing gun battle had cost them a week. The trailing drives were by this time catching up.

Rumour had it that this was to be the last year for Ellsworth. Up to this point it had been the place to take the Texas cattle after the enforcement of the quarantine border. Abilene was then closed to all Texas herds from 1872. The seemingly imminent closure of this trail head meant that if Morgan arrived first with his herd he would be able to nominate his own price.

After they'd left the Chisholm between the Salt Fork of the Arkansas and Pond Creek they struck more trouble at the Arkansas river crossing at Ellinwood. Heavy rains further upstream had caused the river to rise and it remained impassable for a further three days.

Then word arrived that the herd belonging to Bart Williamson out of Fort Worth was only a day behind and closing fast. There were still thirty miles for the Circle M herd to cover.

It was Mike Stall's idea to scatter the Williamson herd. Brolin had protested at first but Morgan had told them to go ahead and do it anyway. Now, with a handful of riders hidden away in a stand of trees, the time had come to stampede the herd.

Williamson's herd was 3,500 head, so their recovery would take sufficient time to allow the Circle M crew to get into Ellsworth first. Brolin had thought about quitting then and there but he knew that his presence would serve to keep Stall in line and prevent things from getting out of hand.

'Move 'em out, Stall.'

'Let's go, boys!' Stall yelled loudly and spurred his mount forward.

Five men, including Brolin, burst from the trees, firing six-guns into the air. Cattle bawled as they started to panic and mill about, confused. A naturally skittish breed, it didn't take a lot to set the longhorns running.

Brolin cursed as the stampeding herd made straight for the Williamson crew's night camp.

'Turn 'em!' he cried out above the thunder of

rumbling hoofs. 'Turn the damn herd!'

None of his crew could hear his voice above the roiling, bawling mass of beef. Brolin spurred his mount savagely and drove it after the leaders of the unstoppable tide. Ahead, in the pale glow of the moonlight, he could make out a rider working frantically to turn the herd away from the Williamson's camp.

After watching the man briefly, it became evident to Brolin that there was no attempt to turn them; rather, the rider was encouraging them to run on. It had become an out-of-control lethal force that could plough through anything in its path.

'Damn it!' Brolin shouted across the mêlée and he forced his horse to go faster.

He managed to gain ground quickly on the leaders and the rider. In the dull silvery glow he could finally identify the man. It was Mike Stall. As he drew level with him he shouted:

'Damn you, Stall! Turn the herd.'

Stall glanced over and snarled, 'Get the hell away from me, Brolin!'

'Turn the damn herd! You'll kill 'em all.'

Stall laughed. The sound was crazy, even maniacal; it turned Brolin's blood to ice water. The man had no intention of turning the mass of longhorns.

As he raced along Brolin drew his six-gun and fired at the leaders, willing them to turn. He fired more shots until his pistol clicked on an empty chamber.

Above the thunder of hoofs, he heard Stall's vicious yell, 'Damn you, Brolin! Damn you to hell!'

Brolin looked across at the wild-eyed Stall, who was matching pace beside him. The look of hatred and rage on the man's face clearly showed his intentions as he brought up his gun and shot Brolin down low in the side.

Brolin grunted audibly as the wind was knocked from him. He felt the bullet tear through flesh but he felt no pain. He slipped sideways in the saddle with the impact. The saddle horn was just out of his grasp, his six-gun slipped through his fingers and fell to the ground.

He hit the earth hard, his head connecting with a stone that protruded from the ground. With his senses reeling the gunfighter tried to rise but failed. His head spun, blurred figures swirled in front of his eyes and, just before he blacked out, Brolin thought he heard the screams of dying men.

'Did you find him?' Stall asked the skinny cowboy.

The man shook his head. 'Nope, not a sign.'

Stall hipped in the saddle. Leather creaked with his movement. He raised a hand to shield his eyes from the glare of the morning sun as he looked across the open country before him. The landscape was seemingly empty: nothing moved.

'Where the hell did you go?' Stall muttered in a low voice.

CHAPTER 1

Northern Pacific Railroad Western Montana. 1885

Red Mike Stall was the meanest son of a bitch ever to walk on two legs. Or so it was said. Most of his men would agree, even if they were themselves outlaws of substantial notoriety like their leader.

From stage hold-ups, bank jobs and cattle rustling, if it happened in Montana the best bet was that Stall and his bunch were likely responsible. They were not limited to Montana, though; they had prices on their heads in Wyoming, Idaho and North and South Dakota.

The bounty for all seven men was upwards of $10,000. Some had tried to collect the cash on the famed outlaws, but all had failed.

Mike Stall was a well-worn thirty-eight years of age, and thickset like a ponderosa pine. His blue eyes and fair-skinned face went typically with the bright-red hair that gave him his name, Red Mike.

He wore a black low-crowned hat over his unruly mane.

Denim jeans clad long legs that contributed to his six-foot-two height, and a dark-blue shirt was worn under a thick jacket, done up to keep out the cold. The chilled high-country winter would soon be upon them. Around his narrow hips he wore a double gun rig, which contained two Colt .45s. Stall rode a tough black gelding he'd stolen the previous year from a ranch over in Idaho.

The outlaws on their mounts sat motionless atop a tree-lined ridge and looked out over a winding, roiling mass of white water known as Elk River. It snaked through a wide gorge topped with a variety of tree species, among them Douglas fir and ponderosas, most of which stood 200 feet high in this part of the pristine wilderness.

There were also lodgepole pines, red cedar with its aromatic scent and spruce trees of varying heights.

Beside the river ran the outlaw's target. The Northern Pacific Railroad tracks followed the course of the Elk river and went on through Fremont gorge.

On the opposite riverbank the escarpment rose steeply, presenting a wall of scarred granite.

'Damn, it's cold!' moaned Jack Murphy as he drew his fur-lined jacket tighter around himself. 'When is the train meant to be comin' through, anyway?'

Murphy was thirty-one and had come to Montana by way of Kansas, where a posse with a rope had hounded him out of the state. He was five-ten tall, of average build, with light-coloured hair and brown eyes.

Stall looked up at the towering mountains and noted that their peaks were becoming shrouded in cloud. Snow comin', he thought to himself.

'Soon,' he said in reply to Murphy. 'Now shut up and stop gripin'.'

The outlaw bit his lip and looked across at the young man called Kansas.

Kansas was twenty-six and, despite his name, he hailed from Colorado. He was a fast-gun who stood five-eleven with a slim build. Blond hair was tucked under a brown Stetson adorned with a silver hatband, which shaded his pale-blue eyes. He favoured a nickel-plated Colt and rode a buckskin horse with a black mane and tail. Like the other outlaws, he was rugged up against the cold weather.

'He's right, Mike,' Kansas allowed. 'It's gettin' damn cold settin' here on this ridge.'

'Don't you start whinin' too,' the outlaw leader snapped. He looked along the line of riders. 'What about you lot? Care to have a cry?'

The other men, Blaine, John Ross and Wallace, ignored the barb and kept their eyes fixed on the rail line below. Blaine, at thirty-five, was the oldest of the remaining outlaws, second only to Stall. He was six feet tall and solidly built with dark hair and eyes. Stall's steely gaze settled on Wallace who sat atop a sturdy chestnut horse.

'You know what you have to do, Wallace?'

'Sure.'

'Well, make sure you're there.'

Wallace's mission was to take the horses once the others were on the train, make contact with the seventh outlaw, West, then ride and meet up with the train at High Point.

High Point was a ghost town at the end of a rail spur, nestled in a draw between two ridge lines. It was the product of a silver boom and had sprung up virtually overnight. After the silver had played out the town's inhabitants had moved on, leaving behind them buildings, mines, equipment and the rail spur that had been used to freight the ore out.

The train's whistle was a plaintive sound as it echoed throughout the gorge. The outlaws turned their attention to their left. The large white plume was highly visible as the train worked its way along the shiny rails of the main line. Foaming white water of Elk River rushed alongside, racing against the slow progress of the iron horse.

'There's our signal boys,' Stall informed them. 'Let's go. Wallace, you make sure you're there with West. You don't show for any reason, you'd best be dead. 'Cause if you ain't, you'll be wishin' you were.'

'Don't you worry none, Mike,' Wallace reassured

the outlaw boss. 'We'll be there.'

Stall dug his heels into his mount's flanks. It moved on to the narrow trail, which wound down the ridge, passed between immense trees and eventually came out near a large rock-slide, where they could hide until the train had passed. After which, they would ride hard to catch up with the rearmost van and climb aboard.

The outlaws let their horses pick their own way along the narrow path. In some sections it sheered away vertically a hundred feet to where jagged rocks sprang from the earth. Twenty minutes later the six of them reached the bottom in plenty of time. The train always travelled slowly through this section of track, as rock-slides were commonplace and had caused more than one derailment in past years.

Hence it was the perfect place for the Stall gang to hitch a ride.

A stand of fir trees beside the rock slide provided excellent cover for the six outlaws, who stayed mounted and tucked their horses in behind the displaced rocks. Then they waited.

Smith sat quietly in his seat and watched the high-country scenery slide silently past as the train puffed slowly through the gorge. He too noticed the cloud around the high peaks and had the same thought as Mike Stall. Snow was coming to the high country.

He felt his seat jerk slightly. The high pitch of a small girl's giggle came from behind him then the sharp, 'Be careful,' of her brother's warning followed.

'Children, behave,' their father chided them. Then to Smith, 'I'm sorry, mister; it's their first time on a train. They're just excited.'

Smith nodded and turned back to face the window. He heard the man say:

'If I have to speak to you again I'll separate you.'

'Sure, Pa,' they replied in unison.

Smith was a man fast approaching middle age at forty-three, but his six-foot-one, thinly built frame still was strong and fit. His suit concealed a body made of whipcord muscle that rippled every time he made a movement.

His hair was black and his brown eyes were set in a weathered face. Instead of wearing a gun like most men out West, Smith wore only a tailored suit, hand-tooled boots and a string tie.

The train rolled on further through the deep gorge, pulling three green-painted passenger cars, a plain stock car and an express car. The locomotive had been built by Richard Norris & Son out of Philadelphia. Made larger than its predecessor with the addition of an added couple of axles and a larger boiler, it could cover longer distances faster.

As the train rounded a curve in the track that allowed for the sweeping river bend, the sun sat at just the right angle to cast the passenger car's shadow out over the jumbled mass of rocks at the river's edge.

Smith frowned, then sat upright in his seat. He stared hard at the shadow below, blinked his eyes then looked again. Two people were moving along the roof of the car in which he was seated. That could only mean one thing.

He was about to lurch to his feet when the rear door of the passenger car crashed open. Smith swung his head round to see what was going on. Coming through the opening were two armed men. Loud cries of alarm erupted as the passengers realized what was happening.

'All right, folks. Just remain seated and everythin' will be just fine,' the first man in through the door warned.

A large middle-aged man dressed in a pin-striped suit stood up. Smith guessed he was from a larger city back East, like St Louis or even further away.

'I must protest, sir . . .' the man started.

The outlaw leader swivelled one of the twin Colts he had clutched in his fists and put a bullet in the man's ample belly. The thunderous noise filled the car with an almost deafening sound. This time screams and shouts rang out through the cordite-filled air of the carriage.

'Keep it down!' the outlaw yelled loudly. 'I said if you all remain seated everythin' would be just fine. Obviously, the man was deaf. Do we have any others on board who are hard of hearin'?'

Nobody answered.

'Good.'

Moans of pain came from the wounded man, who had curled into a fetal position against a woman who, Smith guessed, was his wife. She cried softly and tried to help her husband who was dying before her eyes.

The smell of burnt gunpowder slowly permeated the air.

'Sir?' came an almost timid voice from halfway along the passenger car.

Stall shifted his gaze and pointed his Colt in the direction of the voice.

'What?'

'I . . . I'm a doctor, sir. I would like to see if I can help the gentleman in any way.'

Stall thought for a moment, then he shifted his aim and shot the man again.

'There, now he don't need your help, so shut up.'

The two outlaws walked along the aisle until they drew level with Smith's seat. Stall stopped and looked at him, stared for a time and said:

'Do I know you, stranger?'

Smith looked him in the eye and answered, 'Nope.'

Stall eyed him suspiciously for a moment. 'I'm sure I know you.'

Smith remained silent.

Stall shrugged and the pair moved on, but once at the front of the carriage the outlaw leader paused and said, 'You keep an eye on that feller, Blaine. I know him from somewhere but I can't put my finger on it. If he gives you any trouble, shoot him and be damned.'

Blaine nodded. 'Sure thing, boss.'

Stall disappeared into the next rail car and that was the last Smith saw of him until they reached their destination.

You may think you remember me, thought Smith as he rubbed absently at his side, *but I definitely know you, Mike Stall.*

The train rolled on and Smith could only assume that the outlaws he'd seen carefully picking their way along the top of the rail cars had taken control of the locomotive.

The train emerged from the gorge and picked up speed once more. The rugged terrain flashed past until they were ten miles or so from where the gang had boarded the train; then it left the main line and rolled on to a spur.

Smith at once realized where they were going. Their destination was the ghost town of High Point, an old silver-mining town. A quiet, solitary place.

It concerned him a little because whatever the outlaws had in store for them, it couldn't be good.

CHAPTER 2

Over a period of five years the mining town of High Point had come to life on the back of a silver strike, had lived hard, then died. It was a story similar to that of many boom towns across the West. The last human inhabitant had moved on just two years previously; so, as a ghost town, High Point was relatively new.

Empty false-fronted shops and businesses still lined the streets; the boardwalks, though now silent, were still in as good condition as when the citizens of High Point had last walked them.

The Silver Bullet saloon's sign still hung proudly above double timber doors. Its awning was still erect and intact, as were those of the two other saloons, the Red Garter and the High Point Castle. The Castle had once been owned by an Englishman who had been run out of his home town for sleeping with the wife of a prominent businessman.

A cross could be seen atop the church roof, proudly announcing the building's presence as the train rolled slowly into town. This train was the first rail traffic the town had seen in the three years since the last ore shipment had been freighted out.

Once the train had stopped all the passengers were ordered off and herded into the empty main street.

When they were lined up Stall ordered the newly arrived West and Wallace to take anything of value while he and Kansas blew the MacNeale & Urban safe on board the train. In it they expected to find the $10,000 that they'd been led to believe the train was carrying.

The two outlaws slowly made their way along the protesting line of passengers, taking all they could. A man in his late forties defied the two bandits as he held grimly to a roll of bank notes. West stepped forward and his six-gun rose and fell as it delivered its sickening load to the man's skull. He dropped like a pole-axed steer.

Amid cries of alarm the cold smile of the outlaw broadened as he bent over the prostrate form and ripped the roll from his hand. Then he spat on him for good measure.

Smith felt his ire rise; he wished that he had a gun. Not that it would do him much good. More than likely get him killed. He watched as the two outlaws continued along the line, coming towards him.

He had noticed seven outlaws. Stall and the one called Kansas were in the express car where the safe was located, while three more stood outside, waiting for them to blow it. That left West and Wallace, who were relieving the passengers of their valuables.

A commotion erupted from the express car. Men scattered every which way and Stall and Kansas leapt clear. A thunderous explosion rocked the ghost town and echoed off the surrounding ridges. Flames and smoke belched out of every opening in the car as the dynamite blew. The trick was to use just the right amount, not to use so much as would blow the car off the rails. Now part of the express car's roof had blown off, along with some wall planks.

Some women gasped and every passenger, including Smith, ducked instinctively. Things began to look even worse as a well-dressed man in a dark suit and tie picked up the courage to fight back.

A panicked cry of alarm came from West. Two sharp cracks from a small hideout gun sounded unbelievably loud and the outlaw staggered back, clutching at his chest. Two small red blossoms appeared on the front of his blue shirt.

'Damn it, Wal!' the outlaw cried, bewildered. 'The son of a bitch shot me.'

West sank to one knee, paused as if to rest, then toppled sideways into High Point's dusty main street.

By this time Wallace had his six-gun out. He fired two wild shots. One bullet found its mark and hit the man in the shoulder, knocking him back and causing his next shot to miss its aim. He staggered to his left, in front of the cowering passengers. Wallace fired three more shots; two of the three missed their target but all found flesh.

'Edgar!' a woman wailed hysterically.

From his crouched position Smith looked along the now rapidly disintegrating line of passengers. He saw a woman bending over a small form. It was the boy who'd been seated behind him.

Cries of fear filled the high mountain air as the man, now mortally wounded, fired one last shot. It hit the outlaw high in the right side of his chest. The misshapen piece of lead shredded his lung after ricocheting off a rib, then it exited through his back.

Wallace staggered about like a Saturday-night drunk. There was one live round still left in the chamber of his gun. He tried to raise it once more as his strength ebbed. The six-gun wavered in his hand as he attempted to find another target.

Without giving a second thought for his own safety Smith lunged forward and cannoned into Wallace from the side. The outlaw screamed with pain as both men crashed heavily to the ground.

Smith grappled for the gun, not to use it but to keep the other passengers from harm. He wrenched it from the wounded man's grasp and scrambled back, out of Wallace's reach.

A soft footfall sounded behind him. Before he could react Blaine's six-gun crashed into the back of his head. Bright lights flashed in front of Smith's eyes, then everything went black.

'What the hell is goin' on here?' Stall bellowed. 'God damn it! What was that. . . ?'

Stall's angry gaze dropped to the bodies of his men on the ground. It didn't take a genius to work out that West was dead. He lay unmoving, his eyes open. Wallace was still breathing but those breaths came in gurgled gasps as his injured lung filled with blood.

Stall's rage simmered when he shifted his gaze to the passengers and saw a dead man lying in the dusty street. One arm was outstretched and a small .38-calibre, five-shot hideout gun lay beside the open hand.

Further down the line a woman crouched over the small form of her son. The arms of her husband enveloped her shoulders which heaved in silent sobs as he tried to comfort her. Beside him stood a little girl, softly weeping.

Stall's gaze shifted again and lit upon two more wounded people, both men.

'What the hell happened here?' he snarled at Blaine. The outlaw shrugged his shoulders.

'I don't know. When I got here that feller there,' he pointed at Smith, 'was on his knees and had Wallace's gun. So I cracked him on his skull before he could use it.'

Stall cursed out loud and drew his right-side Colt. He aimed at the unmoving form of Smith and thumbed back the hammer.

'Wait!'

Stall looked up at the short, stout lady who'd stayed his trigger finger. His angry eyes bored into hers.

'He didn't shoot your men.' She pointed at the dead passenger with the gun near his outstretched hand. 'He did. All the man on the ground did was try to stop any more innocent people getting killed.'

Stall let his eyes linger on the woman's face, then he looked back at Smith.

He realized that this was the man from the train who had seemed oddly familiar and had set his mind to wondering.

He frowned. The man's shirt and coat had ridden up in the scuffle with Wallace, exposing pale flesh that bore the large puckered scar of an old bullet wound.

It only took a moment for Stall to realize what he was seeing; then it all came flooding back. He smiled coldly.

'Well I'll be damned! After all this time.'

By now the rest of his men had gathered around. They looked inquisitively at their boss.

'What are you smilin' about?' Kansas asked.

Stall looked around at his men, his smile unwavering.

'Fellers, the man there, all laid out,' he said, stabbing a finger at Smith, 'is none other than Brolin.'

Many of the train's passengers gasped audibly when they realized that they'd been travelling with a wanted killer and gunfighter.

Stall's men looked at him as if he'd gone crazy. After all, the outlaw leader had claimed that he was the one who'd killed the well-known gunfighter.

'I thought you said he was dead.' Kansas gave voice to what they were all thinking.

Stall nodded. 'I thought he was. After I shot him we couldn't find the body. I figured he'd just crawled off some place and died.'

'Are you sure it's him?' asked Jack Murphy.

'Of course I'm damn sure,' Stall snapped. 'I ought to know. See the scar there on his side? That's where I shot him.'

'Well, I guess you can make sure now,' Kansas suggested. 'Put a bullet in his head and be done with it.'

Stall eased down the hammer of his Colt and shook his head.

'No, I got me a better idea. Get him up and get 'em all in that church yonder.'

'Why?' asked Kansas.

'Just do it,' Stall snapped. 'Once you've done that, lock it up tight. I'll be cleanin' out the safe in the express car.'

The outlaw Murphy cleared his throat. 'Um,

about that. . . .'

'What?' Stall's patience was dwindling fast.

Murphy hesitated a moment before he informed his boss of the bad news.

'There is no money.'

'There what?' Stall's voice held a low menacing tone.

'The safe was empty.'

Stall's eyes flashed as he looked about the prisoners.

'Where is the damned express agent?' He located the worried-looking middle-aged man. 'Where is the money? There's supposed to be ten thousand dollars in that safe.'

The man swallowed nervously as the outlaw's steely gaze intimidated him.

'It . . . it never shipped.'

The change in the outlaw boss's demeanour was visible as he grinned at the express agent. A big disarming smile made the nervous man relax a little. Then Stall raised his Colt and shot him in the head.

Amid the cries of alarm and a sudden flurry of movement, Stall shouted aloud:

'Get them in the damn church! Now!'

'All done, boss,' Kansas told Stall, who was sitting on a weathered bench seat that threatened to break under his weight.

Stall looked over and noted with satisfaction the

rusted chain that Blaine had found in the old blacksmith's shop. It was looped through the door handles, effectively sealing the passengers in. He nodded.

'Burn it.'

'What?'

'Burn it to the ground.'

CHAPTER 3

Brolin moaned and rubbed his head as he awoke. He gasped as a flash of pain seared across his scalp and he tested it with a tender prod. His fingers came away clean, but boy, did his head hurt!

'Are you OK, Mr Brolin?' asked a woman's voice.

He froze. He hadn't heard the name in a long while.

Brolin looked up at the woman who'd spoken. She was short and plump and wore a blue calico dress. He recognized her from the train.

'Are you talkin' to me, ma'am?' he asked tentatively.

'Yes, Mr Brolin.'

'I'm afraid you have me confused with somebody else, ma'am,' he lied. 'My name is Smith.'

'That's not what the killer said,' a man chimed in. 'He said it so we all could hear. He said you were Brolin. Said he'd know you anywhere from that bullet scar he put in your hide.'

Brolin sighed and climbed to his feet. He wobbled for a moment, then gathered himself as he leaned on a timber pew.

'Where is Stall?'

'Oh, so you do know him then?' the man asked. His voice dripped with sarcasm. 'Figures. Killers should know other killers.'

Brolin's brown eyes grew cold. He looked directly at the man, who promptly took a step back. He was thin and dressed in corduroy trousers with a matching coat.

'I asked where Stall was?' Brolin said through gritted teeth.

'He's outside somewhere.' It was the woman who answered him.

Brolin turned his attention to her. Unlike the man, she showed no sign of nervousness.

'In case you hadn't noticed,' she continued, 'we're locked in a church.'

Brolin took in their surroundings and noticed that the eyes of nearly everyone in the room were turned to him. Some seemed a little apprehensive but most, he guessed, were curious. He shook off their looks and continued to assess their predicament.

The church was dimly lit. The sunlight that managed to sneak through the cracks in the boarded-up windows was ineffectual in providing much illumination. Many passengers sat on the long timber pews. The space appeared spartan, and lacked the usual accoutrements of a place of worship.

A murmur of voices hummed around the enclosed space, mingled with the sobs of a few. A stifled cry of pain sounded and Brolin saw the doctor tending to a wounded man.

His eyes found the family he'd seen on the train. They were seated on a pew towards the front of the church, the man held his wife while the little girl rested her head on her mother's back. Brolin felt his anger surge back when he remembered the body of the small boy as it lay in the street. He turned back to the woman.

'What happened while I was out of it?'

The woman went on to tell him of the events that had unfolded while he was unconscious. Brolin frowned. Why would Stall refrain from killing him? With what he knew of the killer, from their first encounter up until now when he'd shot the train passengers, it didn't make sense that he should still be alive. He couldn't work it out. Unless. . . ?

'Fire!'

That one word had an immediate effect on everyone locked up in the High Point church. Brolin pushed his way through the crowd of people who'd turned to look to where the cry had come from. The cacophony of anxious voices rose as fear gripped everyone.

Brolin looked at the twin doors of the main

entrance. Smoke swirled beneath them and filtered through the tiny gaps in the doors. He put his shoulder to the oak doors and pushed. They barely moved.

He drew back, then hit them with force. Again with hardly any effect. The rattling sound from the other side told him all he needed to know. Stall and his men had chained the doors shut.

Brolin looked behind him and shouted at a group of men who were standing and watching his ineffectual efforts.

'Give me a hand. The doors are chained shut.'

His words brought more gasps and cries of alarm from the other onlookers but also spurred the men on to come to his aid. Six stepped forward and put the combined weight of their shoulders into the drive at the doors.

The doors snapped back against the chain but it held fast. Though rusted, the iron links were still strong. Another attempt produced a similar result.

'Get something we can use to prise it open,' Brolin ordered.

Two men moved through the crowd to a pew and proceeded to break it up. When they had finished one man scooped up a long piece of four-by-two. They figured that if they could prise it into the small gap between the doors they might be able to lever them open.

'Look! Over there!' This time the cry came from a woman.

Heads turned and the horror of their situation redoubled when they saw a new source of smoke.

'Oh my God! There's another over here!' a man cried.

So that was it, thought Brolin. Stall had set multiple fires, knowing the old church would burn to the ground rapidly and take all inside with it. He'd almost killed Brolin once. By hell, he wasn't going to give him the opportunity to succeed this time!

'Everybody spread out. Check the walls. See if you can find anything – any gaps.'

The crowd dispersed as people went to search along the walls of the building to look for any means of escape. The church was filling with smoke and people began to cough as the acrid fumes burned their throats and lungs.

'I can't find anything,' a man shouted.

'Me neither,' cried another.

A loud crack sounded through the smoke and Brolin turned to look at the source of the noise at the main doors. Despite the thickness of the piece of timber they'd been using, it had snapped neatly in half.

'Oh no,' he heard a young lady cry in despair. 'We're going to die. Burn to death.'

'The hell we are!' Brolin uttered softly. The snap of the timber had given him an idea.

'You men,' he bellowed, 'come with me.'

The men followed him across to another pew.

'Pick it up and carry it over here.'

The men lifted the pew and followed Brolin to the nearer side wall. He heaved another pew out of the way, clearing a passage for them. He pointed at a place on the wooden wall, then ordered them:

'Hit it there. Use it like a battering ram.'

The six men now swung the pew back then brought it forward, using all the strength they could muster. It crashed into the wall with a loud bang. The wall trembled under the assault but remained intact.

'Do it again.'

Back, forward, bang.

'Again.'

Back, forward, bang.

'Again.'

This time a loud crunch greeted their ears as the pew came apart in their hands.

'Damn it!' Brolin shouted. 'Grab another.'

They cast aside the shattered fragments and picked up the pew that Brolin had pushed aside. They went at the wall vigorously once more.

Brolin looked away to check on the progress of the fire. The main doors and the rear wall and roof were well alight. Smoke hung thickly in the air and the erstwhile passengers had squeezed themselves into one small area near the altar.

There came a groan of tortured timber, a loud crack, then a beam near the entrance gave way and a section of the roof caved in. Small roof slats, well alight, and hot chunks of smouldering wood fell to the floor in amongst the pews.

The fire had spread fast as it fed on the church's tinder-dry wood. Brolin turned back to the fatigued men. He rushed across and pushed one of them aside so as to lend his own weight to the makeshift battering ram.

'Come on!' he roared at them, then he coughed violently as he inhaled a lungful of blue-grey smoke.

More roof caved in and crashed to the floor. Frightened screams echoed throughout the smoke-filled room as the passengers huddled ever closer together.

Three more times the pew hit the wall and achieved nothing. The wall remained an immovable barrier, a seemingly insurmountable obstacle between them and freedom. Brolin looked up and saw the orange-red flames as they reached out across the roof, giant tongues the seemed to inhale the dry wood. If the wall didn't give soon they would all die.

'Come on, you son of a bitch, break!'

The fear of imminent death spurred them on. It was a final, desperate plea. Then at last the planks splintered as the pew struck the wall. It had made only a small dent but it was enough to give them hope.

With renewed vigour they hit the wall again. This time the damage was more pronounced. They rammed at the wall over and over again until daylight shone through a narrow gap of a fallen plank. Brolin let the pew go and rushed forward. He drew back his leg and with the sole of his boot he kicked at the other damaged wall planks until he'd created a space large enough for people to squeeze through.

'Go!' he urged the passengers. 'Everybody out through here.'

A steady stream of frightened people squeezed through the gap, out to the sweet fresh air. The wounded were helped out after the women and children and were followed by the men.

Once the seemingly last person had made his way out Brolin looked back to make sure everyone was safe. He noticed the lady in the blue calico dress still lying on the floor of the church. He hurried to her side. She was semi-conscious from smoke inhalation.

Brolin tucked an arm under her and used all of his strength to lift her to her feet.

'Come with me, ma'am,' he encouraged her. 'This ain't no place to hang around.'

He got her to the opening where the air was clearer and sweeter, then guided her through the gap. Once she was safe Brolin followed her out into the fresh air.

With a groan and a crash, the inevitable collapse occurred and the church roof came down, showering dust, sparks and debris in all directions.

CHAPTER 4

'Thank you, Mr Brolin,' the lady gasped out as she regained her breath following the collapse of the church and her close call.

Brolin nodded at her and smiled. White teeth showed bright against his blackened features.

'It was mighty hairy there for a minute, ma'am.'

'Mary,' the woman said.

'Ma'am?'

'My name,' she explained. 'Since you just saved my life, the least I can do is tell you my name.'

'Well then, Mary, you'd best call me Brolin. Drop the mister.'

'Agreed.' She smiled back at him.

'Do you feel OK?' he asked.

She nodded, 'I'm fine. Could use some water. You?'

'Good enough for what I have to do next,' he allowed.

Mary thought for a moment, then said: 'You're

going after them, aren't you?'

Brolin nodded. 'Just as soon as I can.'

'But why?' she asked, concern etched on her face. 'You're only one man.'

Brolin turned and looked to where the now smaller family of only three members were huddled around the little boy's body.

'That's why,' he explained. 'Because if Stall and his gang are allowed to continue their reign of terror, so much more of this will happen. Besides, I owe him for what he did ten years ago.'

'For what he did?'

'Remind me to tell you about it if we ever meet up again,' Brolin said.

She watched him walk off down the road and knew that when he left she would never see him again.

Brolin walked along the dusty street to where the two dead outlaws lay. Stall had taken the time to collect the bag of valuables but nothing more.

From Wallace he took a gun-rig. In the holster was a Remington single-action Army model. It was a .45-calibre six-gun. The loops on the gunbelt were all but full. He strapped it on and tied it down to his thigh using the rawhide thongs at the bottom of the holster. He adjusted it until it felt reasonably comfortable.

After so much time without one, the weight felt unfamiliar but he knew he would get used to it. It would soon feel like an old friend.

From West, he also removed the gun-rig. His weapon of choice was a double action Colt Lightning which also took .45-calibre ammunition. He took the outlaw's low-crowned, flat-brimmed hat and put it on. It was a little snug but would do the job.

Brolin stood erect and slung West's gunbelt over his shoulder. He looked down at the dead outlaw. Flies buzzed about his face and crawled in and out of his open mouth.

'Mr Brolin?'

Brolin turned and saw the man from the train who'd lost his son.

'What can I do for you?' he asked sombrely.

'The lady, Mary, she said you were going after the outlaws who . . . who killed my boy. Is it true?'

Brolin nodded.

'I'm coming with you,' the man said determinedly.

'No,' Brolin shook his head, 'you ain't.'

'Brolin, they killed my boy,' the man pointed out. 'So I'm goin'. With or without you.'

'What's your name?'

'Emmett King,' the man told him.

King was around thirty years of age, Brolin guessed. He wore a suit and was a solidly built six-feet-tall man with brown hair and eyes.

'Don't you think you should stay with your family, King, in their time of need?' Brolin reminded him.

'We live in Black Rock Falls,' King stated. 'My wife has family there. They'll take care of her and Elsie until I return.'

Brolin recognized the name. It was the next town on the main line. He could see the determination on the man's face and knew it would be a waste of time trying to dissuade him.

'What do you do in Black Rock Falls?' Brolin asked.

'I own a dry-goods store,' King confessed; he knew what Brolin was about to say.

'Have you ever killed a man?' Brolin asked flatly. 'I mean, looked him in the eye and shot him down? Or how about shot a man down from a distance with a rifle, coldly and without warning?'

'No,' King mumbled.

'Well, if you come with me that's what you'll have to do.' Brolin was blunt. 'These men are killers. If we're to have half a chance to stop them you will need to think like them and become a killer like them. I've lived their life, King. I'm not proud of it but I know what it takes to stop men like that.'

The store owner bowed his head in shame at his own hesitation and remained silent.

'I'm sorry about your son,' Brolin said softly. 'But your wife needs you. Now more than ever. Go home. I'll get Stall and his men for you. Believe me when I say I can do it.'

King's expression grew hard and he looked up at Brolin. His eyes blazed with fire when he said in a low menacing tone,

'No. I'm coming with you. I want to be there when they pay for what happened to Edgar.'

Brolin took the gunbelt with the Colt Lightning down from his shoulder.

'Here,' he said and held it out. 'If you're coming with me you'll need this.'

King took it and strapped it around his waist. He fiddled with it until he was comfortable.

'Don't shoot yourself with it,' Brolin warned him. Then he left him standing there.

As luck would have it, in their rush to leave the ghost town Stall and his men had left behind the two dead outlaws' horses, which still stood where they'd been hitched.

One was a buckskin, the other a bay. They had their saddles and other gear on them, which included two saddle boots complete with rifles.

The rifle on the bay was a Winchester 1866 model with an octagonal barrel and was chambered for a .44-calibre cartridge. The buckskin had an 1874 Sharps carbine. It also came with an octagonal barrel but was chambered for a .45 round.

Brolin decided that the Sharps was way too much gun for a greenhorn to handle and made up his mind to ride the buckskin himself.

He went through saddlebags and found spare ammunition. Both horses had canteens with water on them. Food they could get on the trail. In the high country grub was easy enough to come by.

Brolin looked at the sun. The great orange ball was starting to sink towards the western horizon. He wouldn't be able to track Stall and his bunch at night, so he decided to leave at first light.

He found King saying goodbye to his wife and daughter. The woman saw Brolin's approach and moved to meet him.

Dora King was twenty-nine. She was almost as tall as her husband and slim. Her long black hair resembled a bird's-nest after the day's events. Brolin guessed she had a pretty face but, under the black soot, he couldn't quite tell. Her large brown eyes were red-rimmed and tears had made tracks in the soot on her cheeks. Her pale dress was torn in a couple of places but when she faced Brolin she held her head up and looked him in the eye.

'Dora, don't.' King tried to stop his wife from what she was about to say.

'Mr Brolin,' she started, her voice a little hoarse from the smoke. 'I've heard all about you and what you have done. I don't like that you are willing to take my husband along with you on this revenge ride. It is said you are a cold, heartless killer and perhaps you will succeed in your quest. But I want you to stop my husband from going with you. After today, if we . . . if we lost him too, I don't know if I could go on.'

'Dora, please. . . .' King pleaded.

Brolin looked at King then back to his wife: his unwavering gaze met hers.

'Ma'am, I'm sorry but I can't do that,' he apologized. 'There are some things in life a man just has to do, even if it means he could get himself killed doin' it. Now I'm sorry about your boy, I really am, but if your husband's set on comin' along I'm not going to stop him. I'll even welcome his help. All I can say is I'll do everything in my power to make sure he comes back home to you and your little girl.'

Dora burst into tears once more. Not tears of sadness, but ones born of frustration and fear. Her eyes sparkled with fire as she looked Brolin squarely in the eye.

'Damn you!' she shouted at him before she turned to her husband. 'And damn you too!'

She whirled around and stormed off.

King gave Brolin an apologetic look.

'Thank you.'

'Don't thank me,' Brolin snapped. 'I agree with her wholeheartedly. You don't belong on this trip and there is a good chance you could get killed. But we may as well get one thing straight. If I am to get you back home to your wife and family alive, you'll do what I say, when I say it. Or I'll shoot you myself.'

Brolin left King standing there, open-mouthed, to ponder on his last words.

*

Though the dynamite blast had damaged the express car it was still operational, therefore the engineer and fireman decided that the train would be safe enough to use to get everyone back into Black Rock Falls. Shortly after dark the train pulled out of High Point. Brolin and King stood and watched it go.

After the night had swallowed the locomotive's sounds, an eerie silence descended and joined a biting cold. Brolin and King walked over to the church where flames still licked amongst the rubble and the warmth radiated was most welcome. While they sat King suddenly asked:

'Why are you doing this? Going after the outlaws, I mean.'

'Let's just say I owe Stall for what he did.'

'Did you do what they say?'

'You've heard the stories,' Brolin said. 'What do you think?'

'I want to hear it from you,' King told him.

'Why?'

'I'd like to know the man I'm going to be riding with.'

'It's a bit late to be worryin' about that now, ain't it?' Brolin asked.

'From what I've observed so far,' King explained, 'I rather think the stories I read in the paper are somewhat exaggerated.'

'There you go,' Brolin said in a mocking tone. 'You never should believe what you read in papers.'

'So tell me then,' King urged.

Brolin thought about it for a moment, then sighed.

'All right. You know the part about the herd we was drivin' to Ellsworth. The owner wanted to reach there first to get the best price on offer. He'd heard it was to be Ellsworth's last year as a railhead. So he hired me to ramrod the drive. Lots of things went wrong on the trail and the trail herds behind us were catchin' up. Stall rode with us on the drive and he was the one who came up with the idea to scatter the herd closest to us. I didn't like the idea but thought it better if I went along to keep an eye on things. The last thing we were told was to steer the herd away from the night camp.'

Brolin paused as he remembered what had happened next.

'When they scattered they started runnin' straight at the camp. Stall was at the head of the herd and instead of tryin' to turn 'em he let 'em run on. I tried to turn 'em but he shot me. I fell out of the saddle and hit my head. Don't remember much after that but when I woke up I was nowhere near where I was supposed to be and had no idea who I was.

'I staggered around for days until I was picked up by a small wagon train headed west. They took care of me and by the time my memory came back it was too late. According to the stories I was dead, so I decided to stay that way. If I'd gone back I would have been lynched.'

'What about Stall? He was there too.'

Brolin shrugged, 'I don't know, I've heard the stories about him but that's it. I figure he was the one who blamed me for it all. But I don't know what happened to him after that night. I'm not surprised he turned killer like he did. He was killin' crazy the night he ran the herd through the camp.'

'So what happened next?'

Brolin looked at him thoughtfully then said, 'After that we turned in and got some sleep. We have a long day comin' up tomorrow.'

King knew enough to let it go. He did as Brolin suggested and got ready for sleep.

CHAPTER 5

'What are we goin' to do now, Mike?' Kansas asked cautiously.

Since their departure from High Point Stall had been submerged in a dark mood. He'd lost two men and there was nothing to show for their efforts.

From the ghost town the outlaws had headed south-west and further into the high country. Now they were camped beside a stand of aspen, the straight silver trunks with small black markings stood luminescent in the pale moonlight. Nearby, a narrow stream burbled along as it snaked through the valley.

Further up the valley the howl of a lonesome wolf drifted along on the chilled night air. Stall lifted his gaze from the camp fire's dancing orange flames.

'We're goin' over to Lazy River,' he said in a low voice.

'But we'll have to go through Bullet Pass,' Kansas pointed out.

'Yeah, so? What's your point?'

'You've seen the snow on the peaks.'

'I have,' Stall acknowledged. 'What? Are you scared of a little snow?' he scoffed.

Bullet Pass was a narrow gap between two granite-faced peaks. The old mountain men had a saying that in winter you needed to travel at the speed of a bullet to get through before the next avalanche.

'Well, don't you worry none, Kansas,' Stall went on. 'I'll hold your hand for you until we get through if it will make you feel better. Besides, it ain't full snow season yet. I doubt there's enough up there to make a blasted snowman with.'

'What are we goin' to do in Lazy River?' asked Ross, whose hands were wrapped around a steaming cup of coffee.

'We're goin' to hit the bank there before we head north to Canada. Once we get over the border we'll circle to the east and cross back over into Dakota. Then we're goin' after the prize. A big pay-day that'll see us settin' pretty for a while.'

Now he held their interest.

'Where might this big prize be?' asked Blaine.

'We're goin' to the Black Hills.'

The shock on Blaine's face was obvious. 'The hell you say!'

'The Homestake mine is shippin' gold out like you wouldn't believe,' Stall explained. 'So I figured I wanted to get me some of that action.'

'We can't go robbin' the Homestake,' Blaine warned. 'Do you know how many guards they have on their shipments?'

'You let me worry about it,' Stall said, trying to allay the outlaw's fears. 'I'll get us some more help before then. It won't matter how many ways we have to split the gold, we'll have enough to be rich ten times over.'

Stall's men liked the sound of it, though every one of them was hoping the outlaw boss knew what he was doing.

'Where do you think they're headed?' King asked as the narrow trail began to climb.

'Bullet Pass,' Brolin answered without looking back.

This was their third day on the outlaws' trail and they'd still not gained any ground on them. King, being a townsman, was unused to the rough going in the saddle. Here in the wilderness he was a hindrance, serving only to slow Brolin down.

'Is that a town?'

'Nope.'

'What is it then?'

'It's what it says,' Brolin explained, his impatience close to the surface. 'It's a pass. The trail runs between two peaks, above the snow line.

From there it runs down into a valley to the town of Lazy River.'

'I've heard of that town,' King said, sounding pleased.

They rode on in silence. The horses picked their way along the rugged trail as it climbed up through rocky outcrops and stands of aspen with leaves of gold, yellow and red. Tall pines cast long shadows across the steep slope that fell away to their left.

'Why do they call it Bullet Pass?'

The question came from nowhere. One moment there was silence, the next, the words tumbled from King's mouth. Brolin's lips thinned with frustration.

'It's called that because if we don't go through it fast enough a whole lot of snow could fall on our heads.'

'You mean an avalanche?'

'Of course I mean an avalanche.'

'Oh,' was King's only reply.

They passed the snow line in the early afternoon. The landscape of greens and golds transformed suddenly into pristine white. A blanket of snow covered almost everything there was to see. With it came a bone-chilling cold. As Brolin and King did not have suitable clothing as protection they were forced to use the blankets from the bedrolls behind the saddles to keep warm.

Mid-afternoon saw the pair enter the pass. It was narrow and two sheer rock walls rose up high on both sides. At the top there was an overhang of snow and ice. It clung precariously to the cliff face. A light snowfall was adding to the build-up and Brolin guessed it wouldn't be long before the overhang gave way.

The horses plodded through the snow, heads bowed. White powder settled upon both man and beast.

A loud crack caused Brolin to look up sharply. At first, a few small pieces of ice fell through the void and crashed into the pass. These were followed by another loud crack and Brolin knew that things were about to become really interesting. He hipped around in the saddle.

'King! Ride, damn it! It's coming down.'

Alarmed, King's first instinct was to look up. What he saw chilled him to the core. A massive chunk of ice and snow had broken away from the overhang and begun its perilous fall.

King froze, his face a mask of terror.

'King!'

The sound of his name being shouted snapped him from his daze. He kicked the bay horse brutally in the flanks to get it to move. The horse lifted its head and lunged forward, hindered by the knee-deep snow as it tried to break into a gallop.

Frantically Brolin went to work on the buckskin

as the pair fled for their lives. A great rumbling sound filled the pass as the white wall of death thundered down the mountain. Large chunks of ice and snow tumbled around the men as they rode desperately to keep ahead of the oncoming mass.

Gradually the horses picked up speed as they fought the soft, treacherous snow. The noise became louder and louder until there came a loud *whump* as the avalanche hit bottom. Hundreds of tons of snow, ice and rocks landed far too close behind King and his bay for comfort. A great white cloud sprayed out, covering both men in a layer of damp powder.

Then the thunderous roar abated and Brolin dared to risk a glance over his shoulder at the pass. There things were beginning to settle. When the two men finally pulled up they were through Bullet Pass and out of danger.

'Are you OK?' Brolin asked a pale and shaking King.

'Uh . . . yes. Yes . . . I think so,' King gasped breathlessly. 'That sure was close. I thought I was goin' to die.'

'It gets easier from here,' Brolin told him. 'Once we get below the snow line we'll make camp, then tomorrow we should make Lazy River.'

'Are you sure you want to go ridin' in there? You bein' wanted and all,' King reminded him.

Brolin considered the question, then brushed

any concerns to one side. If Stall had passed through Lazy River then he, Brolin, would be the last person anyone would be concerned about.

CHAPTER 6

Five men and three women cowered fearfully in a darkened corner of the Lazy River Savings & Loan while Stall beat the manager about the head with his gun barrel.

'I warned you, didn't I?' he snarled. 'I told you not to mess around and play me. But you didn't listen.'

The six-gun rose and fell three more times; then the manager slumped to the floor and didn't move. Blood poured from multiple lacerations to the middle-aged man's face.

Stall stood over him, panting from the exertion he'd put into the beating.

The five outlaws had ridden into town separately. Blaine and Ross met up at the Deuce High saloon while Kansas and Jack Murphy lounged around the streets trying to look inconspicuous as they waited for Stall.

Once the outlaw leader had arrived four of

them converged on the bank, while Ross waited across the street with the horses.

'Damn it, Mike! You've killed him,' stated Kansas.

Stall shrugged his shoulders. 'Yeah, well.'

He looked over at the cowering forms in the corner and spotted the bank clerk.

'You,' Stall's voice thundered in the bank's close confines. 'Get the damn safe open. And make it quick, unless you want to end up like your boss here.'

The clerk, a small thin man with buck teeth, tentatively edged forward. Stall stepped close to the frightened man and grabbed his collar. Then he half-dragged, half-carried him behind the counter and stopped at the safe's door.

'Get it open. Now.'

The clerk fumbled with the lock on the Diebold-manufactured safe. His hands trembled and he had to pause to gather himself together.

'How's it look outside?' Stall called out to Blaine.

'It's OK so far,' Blaine answered impatiently. 'Though I think some folks are startin' to get wind somethin' is up.'

Stall turned back to the clerk, who was starting to swing the heavy door open.

'Good, now get out of the way,' he ordered. 'Blaine, stay at the window. Kansas, give me a hand.'

That left Murphy to watch the prisoners.

Stall and Kansas hurriedly started to fill small flour sacks with as much money as they could lay their hands on.

'How much you reckon is here?' Stall asked.

'Has to be two or three thousand,' Kansas guessed.

'Yeah. That's what I was thinkin'.'

'Hey, Mike,' Blaine called to his boss.

'What's up?'

'You'd better hurry. I got a feller comin' across the street wearin' a badge.'

'Damn it!' Stall cursed out loud. 'We'll be out shortly.'

The pair roughly stuffed the last few bills into the sacks and emerged from behind the counter just in time to see the door open to admit the man Blaine had warned them about.

Shock registered on the deputy sheriff's face as he took in the scene before him. The bloodied dead man on the floor, the terrified customers and bank clerk, and the four men who faced him with guns drawn.

'What the hell. . . ?'

It was all the young man could get out. Instinctively he clawed for his Colt six-gun, but before he had it halfway clear of its holster thunder filled the room. The outlaws fired in unison and their bullets ripped the deputy's chest apart. Blood spattered over the large window behind him and the young man's body was hurled violently backwards by the impact. He hit the low glass with tremendous force and fell through it. Shards scattered and the body came to rest outside on the rough plank boardwalk, his boots resting on the sill.

'It's time we left, boys!' Stall shouted amid the screams of some women.

The four outlaws rushed outside, waved their guns in the air and fired indiscriminately. It was a tactic designed to scare and confuse the townsfolk for long enough to allow the robbers a clear getaway. It didn't work. While the women and children of Lazy River hurried from the street, the menfolk responded valiantly and fought back.

They took cover wherever they could find it. Behind a water trough, in an alleyway or behind an upright awning post. They didn't run away and as Stall and his men ran across the street to get to their horses a hail of lead followed their every step.

Stall felt the burn of a bullet as it passed close to his face. Another clipped his jacket, while a third chewed a piece from his hat. Small eruptions of dirt leapt around his feet, splinters were chewed from the woodwork of the false-fronted shops.

Kansas took his time and picked his targets methodically before he squeezed the trigger.

Murphy and Blaine fired at anything that presented a target before Blaine went down with a bullet to his thigh. Murphy came to his aid and helped him over to the horses.

So far the outlaws had been lucky. With all the lead flying around, only Blaine had actually been hit.

Murphy gave Blaine a leg-up into the saddle while Ross, already on his horse, held Blaine's mount steady. Stall and Kansas leapt aboard their mounts whilst keeping a firm hold on the sacks of money. The air was filled with a sound as of angry hornets as the outlaws swung their horses around in the middle of Main Street and pointed them out of town.

A cry of pain drew Stall's attention to Ross, who was hunched over in his saddle.

'Are you OK?' he shouted at the wounded outlaw.

Ross straightened up and Stall could see the red stain high up on the right side of his chest.

Ross winced with pain.

'I'll be. . . .'

That was as far as he got before a second bullet smashed into his head and turned his brain to mush. He toppled sideways from his horse and landed with a sickening thud on the street's hard-packed earth.

'Damn it to hell!' Stall bellowed. 'Come on, let's go.'

The outlaw leader spurred his horse hard and it leaped forward. The others followed his lead and before long all that was left of their passing was the smell of burnt gunpowder and the dead bodies.

When Brolin and King rode into Lazy River the following day the tension in the air was so palpable that the gunfighter started to wish that he'd let King come in on his own.

As they rode warily along Main Street the locals stared at them. Not inquisitively but with apprehension, nervousness, or even, here and there, suspicion. Brolin moved uneasily in his saddle and placed a hand on his Remington's gun butt.

'Is it just me? Or do these people have an uncommon interest in us?' King wondered.

'Somethin' isn't right,' Brolin stated. 'And if I had to guess, I'd say Stall is behind it. So let's just get some supplies and be gone.'

'What are we goin' to do for money?' King asked the obvious question. After all, the outlaws had robbed them of every last cent.

'I've got money. I've a small poke hidden in my boot. That's why Stall's men didn't find it. What they got was loose change.'

They rode along further, past a small hotel, and the Deuce High saloon. On the opposite side was the jailhouse. On the porch in an old rocking-chair was a middle-aged man, cradling a sawed-off Greener. He watched them intently as they passed, then he rose and walked inside.

'Look at that,' King said in a hushed voice.

Brolin turned to look at what had drawn King's attention and saw the bank's smashed front window. He also noticed bullet scars in the woodwork around it and the dark stain on the boardwalk, which he guessed was blood.

'I'd say Stall and his boys stopped here briefly,' Brolin suggested. He looked about and saw more signs of the previous day's gun battle.

Outside the undertaker's he saw an open casket leaning against the wall. Inside was the cold, stiff body of John Ross.

Brolin didn't know his name but he recognized him as one of Stall's men.

'Is that. . . ?' King's question remained unfinished.

'Yeah, it's one of them.'

'Good,' King said in a harsh voice. 'One less we'll have to deal with when we catch up.'

'Over this way,' Brolin said. He pointed to a false-front building with large windows and a painted yellow sign above the awning. It read Emporium.

They guided their horses over to the hitch rail and looped the reins around it. They climbed the steps, walked across the boardwalk and up to the glass panelled door.

'Wait out here,' the gunfighter ordered.

When Brolin swung the door open a small bell tinkled to announce his arrival.

The front of the store was empty, but as he

sidled up to the counter a small, middle-aged man with round features came from a back room to greet him.

He hesitated for a moment when he saw Brolin's gun, tied down low in a familiar style.

'I need some supplies,' the gunfighter announced.

'Yes. . . .' The man stammered nervously, 'W-w-what is it you need?'

'Coffee, bacon, some beans and two boxes of .45 ammunition, a box of .44s and a box of .45s for a Sharps.'

The man nodded, 'Yes sir, that shouldn't be a problem.'

'Also,' Brolin continued, 'I need a couple of slickers and two warm jackets.'

The bell tingled as it announced the arrival of someone else in the store.

'Will that be all, sir?' the owner asked. 'Or will there be something else?'

'That won't be necessary, Charlie,' a deep voice said from behind Brolin. 'Turn around, mister, and keep your hands clear of your hardware.'

Brolin turned slowly, being careful to make sure his hand stayed well clear of the Remington. Standing there with his sawed-off shotgun pointed at Brolin's midriff was the man he'd seen seated outside the jail.

'What can I do for you, Sheriff?' Brolin asked hesitantly.

'That's Deputy,' the man said. 'Deputy Sam Crawley. And you, Brolin, are under arrest.'

CHAPTER 7

Brolin cursed himself for a fool as the steel-barred jail door slammed shut behind him with a loud clang.

'Man, wait until the sheriff gets back and sees what I caught,' the deputy gloated. 'Everyone thought you were dead for sure. Then you turn up here. I saw you in Abilene once. I think it was '74. You took down the Thompson brothers after they gunned a feller on your crew. That's how I recognized you on the way in.'

'Small world. I'm startin' to think it might have been better if I had've stayed dead.'

Brolin looked around the small cell. The back and side walls were of block construction while the front and the wall to the adjoining cell were iron bars. The steel-framed cot against the solid wall was low and the mattress lumpy. Apart from the smell, there was nothing more.

Then something occurred to him. Where was

King? After the deputy had arrested him and taken him outside the store, King was nowhere to be seen.

'Why here?' Crawley's voice broke into his thoughts.

Brolin frowned and looked at him. 'What?'

'What brings you here?'

'Will it make a difference if I tell you?'

Crawley shrugged. 'Nope. I was just curious is all.'

'I'm chasin' the feller who robbed your bank yesterday.'

The deputy moved in close to the bars, his expression hardened. 'How do you know our bank was robbed?'

'Not hard to tell, really,' Brolin said drily, and went on to explain why. 'The bank has a smashed window, bullet scars in the wall and your undertaker has one of them on public display outside his front door.'

'What are you chasin' 'em for?'

'They held up the train I was on four, five days ago,' Brolin explained. 'Killed some passengers. One happened to be a small boy.'

'He kin of yours?'

'Nope.'

'Then why bother?'

'I owe their leader.'

'Do you know who their leader is?' Crawley asked.

'Mike Stall.'

'Red Mike Stall?'

'Yeah.'

The deputy whistled slowly. 'The witnesses only said his name was Mike. Man, the sheriff is goin' to have a grizzly by the tail if he catches up with him.'

'You want to let me out so I can go after him?'

Crawley looked at him and smiled broadly.

'Nope.'

'Yeah, well. It was worth the try.'

King watched the jail from across the street. He sat on a rough plank seat outside the barber's shop. He was trying to work out what to do and every solution he could think of to the current problem led to the same conclusion: he had to bust Brolin out of jail.

Although he was torn between that and going on alone, he reasoned that the latter would only get him killed. No, the only way to get his revenge against Stall and his gang hinged on Brolin's being with him. So he had to be ready if he was going to get him out.

King moved off, determined to do just that.

'Stand back against the wall,' Crawley ordered. He waited for Brolin to move.

Brolin stepped back a couple of paces and watched as the deputy unlocked the cell door. The keys rattled against the metal briefly, then the door swung open with a soft squeak.

With the sawed-off shotgun trained on Brolin's midriff, Crawley stepped into the cell and bent at the knees to pick up the tray on which the food had been brought in.

The gunfighter stayed where he was. He knew better than to buck twin barrels loaded with certain death.

The deputy scooped up the tray and backed away through the open door. He placed the tray on a small table, then locked the door again.

'Enjoy the meal?' he asked conversationally.

'I've had worse,' Brolin answered with a shrug.

In fact, the meal had been quite good. It wasn't much: just steak and beans, but it tasted great on an empty stomach and had been washed down with a lukewarm cup of bitter black coffee.

'I sent word over to Black Rock Falls earlier, askin' about the train thing you mentioned,' the deputy informed Brolin. 'The answer came back a while ago confirmin' what you said, so I guess you was tellin' the truth. It was mentioned that you helped save lives while you were there, too.'

'And?'

'And nothin'. You stay right there. Ain't nothin' you can do is goin' to make up for what you did to the trail crew in '75.'

He was about to say more when there was a sound of knuckles rapping loudly on the outer hardwood door.

The door was locked. Crawley approached it and opened a small hinged flap that had replaced the original window. Outside it was dark. Kerosene lanterns placed at intervals along the street provided a dim glow. The night air was chilly and King was rugged up in a coat he'd stolen from an unsuspecting woman's washing-line.

'What do you want?' Crawley asked the stranger who stood outside the door on the boardwalk.

'The barkeep sent me over from the saloon. Said you needed to get over there now. He thinks one of them fellers who robbed your bank yesterday is in there.'

Crawley looked at the stranger sceptically.

'You mean Walter sent you over here?'

'No,' King said. He'd made a point of finding out the barkeep's name just in case the deputy called him on it. 'The feller's name was Smitty. I guess his last name is Smith.'

'Damn it!' Crawley cursed. He turned away from the door and crossed to the scarred wooden desk where he'd left the shotgun. He went back to the door, unlocked it and swung it open. 'If Smitty has got me on some wild-goose. . . .'

He stopped cold when the hard barrel of King's Colt Lightning poked into his midriff.

'Back up,' King ordered through gritted teeth. 'And don't try anythin' smart or I'll blow your spine out your back.'

The stunned deputy backed up slowly. Once

they were clear King closed the door without taking his eyes off Crawley.

'Now, drop the gun on the floor and turn around.'

'You . . . you'll never get out of town,' the deputy stammered.

'Shut up and do what I say,' King hissed.

Crawley let the gun clatter to the wooden floor and turned around as he'd been told.

King stepped forward swiftly and chopped the barrel of his six-gun down on to the back of Crawley's head. The man dropped like a stone. King bent and picked the keys from his belt.

'I was wonderin' where you'd got to,' Brolin said. 'I was beginnin' to think you'd left town.'

'I thought about it,' King said truthfully. 'But I decided I needed you if there was any hope of makin' those bastards pay.'

King unlocked the door and they dragged the unconscious deputy into the cell. Brolin found his Remington in the gun cupboard and strapped it on.

'The horses are outside,' King told him.

'Good, but before we leave town there is one more stop to make.'

A look of despair came over King's face.

'You've got to be joking. As soon as he wakes up he'll start yellin' loud enough to bring half the town runnin'.'

'True.' Brolin nodded thoughtfully. 'Wait here.'

Brolin unlocked the cell, ripped the deputy's bandanna from around his neck and used it as a gag. He then pulled the man's belt free and tied his hands behind his back.

'That'll keep him busy for a while. Now, come on. We need to get them supplies before we go.'

A loud banging brought the storekeeper downstairs. When he opened the door he was not a happy man.

'What the hell. . . ?' The man stopped abruptly and his face fell when he saw who was standing there. He felt the gun muzzle prod at his belly.

'Hi Charlie.' Brolin smiled mirthlessly. 'I've come for my supplies.

Sheriff Ben Dawson was not a happy man either. He was cold, tired and hadn't been asleep for long when suddenly he found himself awake once more.

He and the ten-man posse he was leading were camped out beside a small beaver pond, which was fed water from a clear narrow stream – clear enough to see the rounded rocks on the bottom.

He sat up and stretched out some the kinks caused by sleeping on the hard ground. It might be grassy but it certainly wasn't soft. He looked around the camp. The dull light of the campfire's low orange flame illuminated the men huddled under their blankets, fast asleep. Low snores drifted on the chilled night air and a posse member rolled over and mumbled something incoherent.

Dawson shook his head and swore softly. He frowned; why was he awake again? It was quiet enough, there had been no loud noise or anything to rouse him.

A horse snorted, then they all began to shuffle about. Dawson peered into the darkness. Perhaps a wolf or mountain lion was on the prowl in the dark wilderness.

Suddenly the night split apart with the sound of gunfire. Orange and red stabs of flame erupted from the ends of rifle and six-gun barrels. The impact of each round caused the blanket-covered men's bodies to go into violent spasm. Screams of pain filled the air. A couple of men managed to scramble to their feet after throwing their blankets aside. They got off a few shots before they were brought down amid the throaty roar of a cut-off shotgun.

Dawson overcame the initial shock of it all and lunged at his holstered .38-calibre Navy Colt, which was beside his saddle. He brought it up and began to fire at the gun flashes. After the first couple of shots he was rewarded with a yelp of pain from the darkness.

When the first bullet hit him in the side it felt as though a mule had kicked him. It knocked the breath from his lungs and caused him to gasp for air. The second one hit him just above the belt buckle and made him double over.

Dawson dropped the Colt from his weakening grasp and sank to his knees. His ears still rang with the cries of his men dying amid the sound of murderous gunfire. Then, mercifully, a wave of darkness swept over him and he slumped on to his side.

'Who?' Stall asked Kansas.

'Blaine.'

'Can he ride?'

'I doubt it.'

Stall grunted and walked over to the fire where the others had carried Blaine. The outlaw shivered violently from pain and shock. Stall could see the beads of sweat on the wounded man's brow glistening in the firelight.

'Kansas says you can't ride.' It wasn't a question, just a statement of fact.

'I'll be f-fine,' Blaine stammered.

'Nope. You won't.' Stall's voice was devoid of emotion. 'We can't hang around and wait for you.'

'J-just give m-me a day, Mike,' Blaine gasped. Stall shook his head.

'I'll leave you your canteen and horse. If you start to feel better and manage to get mounted try and catch up.'

Fear flickered across the wounded man's face.

'N-no. What a-about bears or w-wolves? You

c-can't leave me.' Stall shrugged his shoulders.

'It is what it is. See you, Blaine.'

Stall turned. He walked towards the horses but he was brought up short by Kansas and Jack Murphy.

'You can't leave him like that, Mike,' Kansas protested. 'He's one of us.'

'Yeah, Mike,' Murphy put in. 'The critters will eat him alive.'

Stall's voice grew cold. 'If he comes with us he'll slow us down. On the other hand, if you don't like leavin' him here alive then draw straws.'

Kansas's mouth drew into a thin line with the grim realization at what his boss had suggested.

'What for?' Murphy asked, slow on the uptake.

'So you can find out which one of you shoots him in the head. Whatever you decide, make it fast. I'm leavin'.'

Stall turned away. He walked to his horse, leaving both men contemplating what they should do.

CHAPTER 8

Brolin spat on the ground as he surveyed the scene before him. He'd seen a lot of death in his time but you never got used to it. Especially on a scale like this.

The bodies were scattered around the camp, left where they had fallen. Off to the side, King dry-heaved once more; all of his stomach contents were long gone. He straightened up and wiped his mouth on his sleeve.

'How can you just stand there and be unmoved by all of this?'

'Men deal with death in different ways,' Brolin told him as he looked down at the body of Blaine. He had a bullet hole in the centre of his forehead and another in his chest.

A low moan off to his left caught his attention and he turned swiftly, gun in hand. Carefully he edged forward and found the source of the noise. The sheriff was still alive. Somehow the outlaws had missed him when they left, Brolin thought.

'Over here,' he called to King; he knelt down beside the wounded man.

Brolin eased him over gently and looked at the man's wounds. The one in his side showed a small entry wound; nearby was a larger exit wound. The second wound troubled Brolin more than the first.

The sheriff was gutshot and was dying a slow, painful death. Brolin moved the man's shirt aside to take a better look; a hoarse whisper stopped him.

'Don't bother, stranger, I'm done for.'

King crouched beside Brolin.'What can we do?'

The gunfighter looked at him and gave a gentle shake of his head.

'Surely there must be somethin',' King insisted.

'Don't worry yourself none,' the lawman said quietly. 'He knows there ain't nothin' can be done. Not for a wound like this.'

'When did they hit you?' asked Brolin.

'Sometime after midnight,' the dying lawman said. 'I don't know how they crept up on us. We had nighthawks out.'

'How many?'

'Two.'

Brolin nodded. 'I found 'em. Both men had their throats cut.'

Dawson showed no surprise.

'This trail we're on,' Brolin said, 'where does it go?'

'About forty miles north of here is a small town,' Dawson explained. 'It's called Miller's Crossing. It's on the Standish River.'

'I've heard of it,' Brolin allowed.

A wave of pain swept through the lawman; he shuddered violently, then settled once more.

'I know the sheriff there,' Dawson said. 'He's a good man, but he's no match for these guys on his own.'

'Is there another trail Stall and his men could take?'

Dawson looked surprised. 'No. Is that who it was?'

'Yeah.'

Brolin went on to tell him briefly about the train.

'Son of a bitch,' the lawman cursed weakly.

Another, stronger wave of pain coursed through Dawson.

'Mother of God!' he cried out. 'It hurts.'

When the spasm had passed he lay there gasping. Then he gathered himself and looked Brolin in the eye.

'I need you to make the pain stop.'

The gunfighter nodded. 'OK.'

'How are you goin' to do that?' asked King. Brolin looked at him.

'Go and find some branches so we can light a fire,' he said.

'But—'

'Go!' Brolin snapped.

King turned and walked off into the trees to find what he needed.

'Greenhorn?' asked Dawson with a faint smile.

'Yeah, and then some. His little boy was killed by the outlaws.'

'Bad business.'

Brolin nodded. 'Are you ready?'

'Nope, can't say as I am. Mind tellin' me your name?'

'Brolin.'

Recognition sparked in the lawman's eyes.

'You're supposed to be dead.'

'Tell me about it. I will promise you this, though, Sheriff. I'll kill every last one of them damn murderers before I'm through.'

'One more thing: there's Blackfeet about. A band of 'em jumped the reservation over at Fort Shaw. We got word in town a couple of days ago.'

Brolin nodded. 'Thanks. You got anyone?'

'Nope, just me. But if you could get word to Lazy River I'd appreciate it.'

'I'll do it,' Brolin assured him.

When King heard the gunshot he came running out from the trees, his Colt Lightning drawn and ready to shoot. He stopped short when he saw Brolin standing over the sheriff's body, gun in hand and a small wisp of blue-grey gunsmoke drifting from the barrel.

'What did you do?' he shouted. Brolin didn't

look up.

'I did what he asked me to do.'

'Why?' the store owner gasped out. 'What they said about you is true. You're nothin' but a killer.'

The gunfighter whirled about to face King, his eyes blazing.

'If you ever call me that again I'll leave you out here on your own. The man was dyin' and he was hurtin' more than he could stand. So he asked me to end it for him. Nothin' could be done for him. He could die slow or quick. He chose quick.'

King's face had paled under the verbal barrage. His eyes dropped to the shaking Remington, which was pointed in his direction.

Brolin followed his gaze and realized what he was looking at. He holstered the six-gun, turned away and walked off a distance, stopping when he reached the Beaver pond. He reached inside a pocket and took out a small picture. He stood in silence for a few minutes, looking at it.

King swallowed, then asked: 'What are you lookin' at?'

The gunfighter stuffed the picture back into his pocket and looked up at a ridgeline on the far side of the valley.

'Nothin',' he said in dismissal of the question.

King could tell enough from the man's tone not to press the matter. Instead, he asked:

'What are we goin' to do with all these bodies? Are we goin' to put them over the horses and take 'em with us, or what?'

'Leave 'em there,' Brolin ordered.

'We can't just leave 'em for the wolves and bears or God knows what else,' King protested.

'I said leave 'em.'

'Why?'

Brolin sighed angrily; he didn't turn his eyes away from the far ridge.

'All right, listen up,' he snapped, impatience evident in his tone. 'You see the ridge yonder?'

King moved to stand beside him. 'Yes. What about it?'

'Atop the ridge there's a big spruce tree, standin' all on its own. Do you see it?'

'Yes.'

'To the right of it there is a large rock formation and just below that you'll see 'em.'

'See wha . . . yes, I see 'em.'

Brolin guessed there were fifteen Indians or perhaps a few more. They were sitting, watching. He surmised that they were the Blackfeet warriors who'd jumped the reservation, about whom the sheriff had told him. If that was who they were it would mean trouble.

Brolin glanced up at the sun and judged there would be a few more hours before sunset.

'Let's get the hell out of here.'

The two men turned and walked at a brisk pace towards where the horses were quietly cropping grass. Brolin guessed that the Indians would be coming down off the ridge about now, and making a beeline for the camp.

'Leave the posse horses,' the gunfighter ordered. 'With any luck they'll be satisfied with them.'

'And if not?'

'Then pray we can stay ahead of them until the sun goes down and we can give 'em the slip.'

As fate would have it, everything changed an hour later.

'We'll have to make a stand!' Brolin yelled amid the thunder of horses' hoofs. 'If we keep drivin' the horses like this we'll kill 'em.'

When they'd hit the incline up to the ridge their mounts had begun to labour noticeably. The trail climbed steeply ahead, switching back on itself many times as it cut a path through the pines.

Off to his right Brolin saw a steep rock face with a large deadfall at its base. A little to the left was a massive boulder, which would provide adequate cover for the tired mounts.

'This way,' the gunfighter shouted. He guided the buckskin off the trail.

King followed and they ducked beneath low-hung branches of trees until they reached their destination. Brolin tethered the horses behind the boulder, then dug out the spare ammunition from the saddlebags. He removed the Sharps from the saddle boot.

'Grab your Winchester and canteen,' he ordered King, 'and follow me.'

King did as he was told without question and followed Brolin to where he crouched behind a tree. At least with the cliff at their back they would be safe from that direction.

Brolin watched as the Blackfeet warriors came along the trail through the meadow's open expanse. He'd been right, there were fifteen of them. He set out five .45-calibre cartridges for the rifle within easy reach and left the open box next to them. He took a box of .44s for the Winchester and tossed them to King.

'You'll be needin' them.'

'Do we have a chance?' the store owner asked nervously.

'You'll be fine,' Brolin assured him. 'Take your time and try to hit what you aim at.'

As the Indians came on the two men had a reasonably clear field of fire from their vantage point.

Brolin looked at the sun. There was still around an hour before it sank behind the highest snow-clad peaks. If they could hold out until dark they might be able to slip away.

He turned his attention back to the Blackfeet, who urged their horses on. His brow furrowed and he looked down at the Sharps, which was lying across the fallen tree in front of him.

'King, start shootin'.'

'Aren't they still a bit far away?' King questioned.

'I don't think I could hit anythin' at this distance.'

'I don't want you to,' Brolin explained. 'I just want you to make 'em stop and think. Two shots are all you need to fire.'

While King lined up for his first shot Brolin fed a .45-calibre cartridge into the single-shot Sharps. He too lined up on the fast-approaching group.

'Do it.' Brolin spoke calmly.

The Winchester barked and the shot fell short but the rifle's roar had the desired effect and the Indians stopped.

All of them were armed. Some had Spencers, some Winchesters and a couple had newer-model Springfields.

'Again.'

King worked the lever and fired his second shot. It too fell short but the confused Blackfeet warriors remained where they were.

Brolin sighted the Sharps on the foremost rider, took a deep breath, then expelled it slowly. His finger took up the slack on the trigger.

The Sharps slammed back against his shoulder; its deep, throaty roar echoed along the surrounding ridges. The Blackfeet warrior was thrust bodily from the back of his magnificent buffalo horse and blown backwards over its rump.

There came a cry of confusion as the warriors looked down at the half-naked Indian with the fist-sized crater in his back.

Brolin swiftly opened the loading-gate with the

lever and extracted the spent brass cartridge. He replaced it with a fresh round and closed the breech.

He took a bead on the next painted warrior and fired. Through the cloud of blue-grey gun-smoke that belched from the Sharps' octagonal barrel Brolin saw the warrior throw up his arms and fall to the ground.

This time, however, the Indians overcame the shock of what had happened and were spurred into action. They didn't flee, as Brolin had hoped. Instead they set their mounts in a dead run for the ridge.

'Let 'em have it, King.'

The store owner sighted down the ridge and started firing at the oncoming Blackfeet warriors.

As King laid down fire with the Winchester, Brolin reloaded and fired once more. This time the heavy-calibre bullet smashed into the leading horse's head, killing it in mid-stride. It went down on its nose, tossing the rider forward. The warrior landed head first and his neck broke with an audible crack.

Once more the gunfighter reloaded and sighted; when the Sharps bucked again another Indian went down.

Now the Blackfeet were within range of King's Winchester. With his next aim he hit a target. A Blackfeet warrior cried out in pain and leaned to the right, pressing his hand on his side.

The Sharps boomed again. Brolin cursed. The wounded man's horse had shied into the path of the gunfighter's next target. The warrior hauled away to his left just as the Sharps had discharged its lethal load. The shot flew harmlessly past, three feet wide.

At last they reached the ridge's base. They leaped from their horses, ran into the trees and found shelter from the gunfire amongst the rocks and large pines.

'What happens now?' King asked.

Brolin's face took on a grim expression. 'Now things get interesting.'

Kansas hauled back on the reins of his dun horse and stopped in the middle of the trail. Stall pulled back on his reins, Murphy did the same.

'What the hell are you stoppin' for?' Stall snapped impatiently. Kansas looked at him, puzzled.

'Did you hear it?'

'Hear what?'

On cue, the sound reached their ears. It was faint, but it was unmistakable.

'Did you hear it that time?'

Stall nodded. 'Sharps.'

'That's what I figured,' Kansas confirmed.

A period of silence ended when the gunfire started again. Now there was more than just the Sharps to be heard. The faint popping of many shots drifted to them on the wind.

'Someone sure is havin' themselves a whole mess of trouble,' Murphy observed. 'What do you think's happenin'?'

'Who knows?' Stall shrugged. 'One thing is for certain though. I plan on puttin' a lot more territory between us and whatever it is before dark. Come on. Let's go.'

CHAPTER 9

Brolin ducked behind the deadfall as a bullet chewed out a large gouge and sprayed splinters about. Sharp slivers of wood sliced the air as they passed close to his cheek. One scored a line through the darkened stubble of his jawline, which instantly leaked a few drops of blood.

Beside him, King fired the last two rounds from the Winchester and dropped down to reload. Brolin crouched down beside him.

'How're you doin'?' Brolin asked.

'Ask me if we get out of here alive,' King replied, his voice shaky with tension. The gunfighter looked up at the sun.

'Maybe twenty minutes and the sun will be down behind the mountains. Once it starts to get dark we need to get out of here. They'll figure on usin' the dark, too.'

King looked genuinely shocked.

'I thought they don't fight at night.'

Brolin just stared at him; the store owner shook his head.

'No?'

'Day or night, them Blackfeet down there will kill you deader than hell,' Brolin told him. 'So when the sun goes down, be ready.'

A couple more shots ricocheted from the downed tree trunk and screamed off harmlessly into the surrounding forest. Brolin wasn't sure but he guessed that their attackers were now down to seven. He had to give the store owner one thing: King hadn't shirked the issue. When it came down to the wire he had stood up to be counted.

At this point Brolin realized that something was wrong. There weren't enough guns firing. It could mean the Indians were low on ammunition, which was a possibility considering their steady rate of fire up to now, or else they were up to something.

The gunfighter edged up to look down the slope. Two shots were fired, then nothing. It all stopped.

'King, get up here,' Brolin ordered in a low voice.

With a flurry of movement King was there beside him.

'What's wrong?'

Brolin frowned. 'I don't know.'

'They've stopped shooting. Why?'

'Keep your eyes skinned. They're up to something and I don't know what.'

A flicker of movement caught Brolin's eye a hundred yards down the slope, then disappeared. Brolin slid the Sharps over the trunk and sighted along the barrel.

'They're comin' up the ridge,' Brolin whispered hoarsely. 'Get ready. Things are about to get wild.'

Another flicker of movement was followed by several more. Closer they came until one warrior leaped from cover not thirty yards away. He came at them head on.

He howled wildly: a loud, spine-tingling sound designed to unnerve his quarry. Both King and Brolin swung their weapons to bear and the sound of gunfire split the late-afternoon quiet apart. The Indian screamed and was flung back down the slope. No sooner was he down than another jumped up to take his place.

King worked the Winchester's lever and a fresh round slammed into the breech. He swung the rifle around and pulled the trigger.

The .44-calibre slug missed its intended target and flew into the emptiness beyond. Brolin was engaged in reloading the Sharps; when the store owner missed the warrior Brolin was forced to drop the Sharps and go for the holstered Remington.

His hand wrapped around the walnut grips and started a smooth, fluid draw. But it was no good, the warrior was too close. He cannoned into Brolin. The pair crashed to the ground in a tangled heap. Pain shot through Brolin's right arm when he landed on a round rock the size of a goose's egg.

The gunfighter lost his grip on the Remington, which skittered off under a small bush. Now on top of him, the Blackfeet warrior tore at Brolin's throat with both hands, trying to get a grip. Brolin brought up his closed fist and smashed it into the Indian's head. The Indian didn't flinch. Brolin looked into his half-crazed eyes and saw only the prospect of death if he couldn't shake the warrior loose. The warrior's bony fingers finally found purchase and started to squeeze.

In desperation Brolin drove his fingers at the Indian's eyes. He was rewarded immediately when the warrior threw his head back and cried out with pain.

The gunfighter saw the Indian's exposed throat and chopped viciously at it with his hand. The warrior clutched at his own throat as he tried to breathe, his eyes bulging.

Brolin scrabbled on the ground beside him until his hand wrapped around a fist-sized rock. He swung it with all his might and heard a sickening thud as it smashed into the Indian's head.

The warrior's struggles ceased and his eyes opened wide. Their light faded and he died in a sitting position.

Brolin pushed him away and scrambled to find the Remington he'd lost. He found it and dusted it off. He turned to find King crouched behind a deadfall log, not firing his gun.

'Are you OK?' Brolin asked him.

'Yeah, I'm fine. I got two more. How are you doin'?'

Brolin was still panting from the exertion of the fight. 'I'll live.'

'They've gone,' King said, his relief obvious. Brolin shook his head.

'They're still out there. So keep your eyes open.'

He looked up at the sky. Not long until they could leave and slip away from the Blackfeet war party, hopefully without being seen.

The Blackfeet never came. The sun sank below the western peaks and the only living thing the two men heard was the mournful baying of a wolf some miles distant.

'Do you think they've gone?' King asked for the tenth time.

Brolin sighed, frustration creeping in. 'Stand up.'

Without giving the command a thought, the store owner rose to his feet.

'Now what was it you asked?' said Brolin.

'Have they gone?'

'Well, you're standin' up and you're still alive; that ought to tell you somethin',' the gunfighter pointed out. King dropped back down behind cover.

'Damn it! You could have got me killed.'

'You can't die from somethin' what ain't there,' Brolin explained. 'My guess is they figured they'd lost too many warriors and lit out.'

'So you knew before I stood up that they were gone?' asked King, a hint of anger in his voice. Brolin left the question unanswered.

'Come on, let's get out of here before we find out.'

The afternoon sun was still high above the snow-topped, grey-faced mountains that surrounded Miller's Crossing when the outlaws sighted the town. The lower ridges around it were covered in ponderosa, Douglas fir and spruce. A large stand of lodgepole pine came to an abrupt end on the north side of town, while the south side opened out into a vast grassland bordered with the yellows, reds and golds of the silver-barked aspen.

Through the middle of it all, including the town, flowed the Standish River: a narrow, rock-strewn, swiftly flowing watercourse, spanned by a timber bridge that joined the town together.

On the river's south bank lay the bulk of Miller's Crossing, comprising false-fronted shops, the Big Sky saloon and the homes of its citizens. Across the bridge, on the north side, were the other two of Miller's Crossing's saloons: the Lumberjack and the North Country Star. Also on that side was the Silk Purse, the double-storey concern that served as the local house of disrepute. A large lumber mill, which consumed a constant supply of timber brought down from the mountains, lay further along the riverbank.

'Are we goin' to wait until after dark to ride through, like last time we was here?' Kansas asked Stall.

The outlaw sat on his black mount, thinking, lips pursed. His gaze ran over the buildings in the distance as his mind ticked over for a long moment. Then he spoke.

'No. We're goin' to hang around for a while.'

Kansas and Jack Murphy shot each other concerned looks. Murphy frowned questioningly and was answered with a shrug of Kansas's shoulders.

'Are you sure that's wise?' the outlaw finally asked. 'What about the law?'

'What about the law?' Stall replied, not breaking his concentration from the view before him.

'We've already had our share of trouble lately,' Kansas pointed out. 'Oh – and in case you haven't noticed, we've thinned out some.'

Stall turned and stared at Kansas, giving a look that Kansas knew spelled trouble.

'You let me worry about the law,' Stall said in a low voice that held menace and let the pair know his decision would not be questioned. 'Besides, we need supplies. And I want a drink.'

Looks of resignation passed between Kansas and Murphy. This could only end in trouble.

*

The three outlaws rode casually into Miller's Crossing's bustling main street amid looks of curiosity from the town's citizens. The unshaven, trail-weary men drew attention, as did most strangers.

Lined both sides with a plank boardwalk, the main street led into the town's centre, where a massive ponderosa stood. It was a scarred giant, well on the way to being 180 feet tall. A square of hitch rails fenced it off.

From this point the street forked. One branch, to the right, led past some more false-front businesses while the one to the left inclined gently towards the bridge, leading to the less salubrious part of town.

'Are we goin' in there?' Murphy asked, pointing out the Big Sky.

'Nope,' Stall shook his head. 'Over the river.'

A line of seven freight wagons rumbled across the bridge, loaded with lumber. Teams of four large powerful horses hauled each of them. They moved ponderously along the rutted main street and forced the outlaws to move their mounts to one side. Once they had passed Stall eased his black out into the street.

'Come on. I want a drink.'

The outlaws rode across the bridge to the north side. Beneath the bridge flowed the roiling mass of white water known as the Standish River. Large round boulders protruded above the surface, worn smooth with the passage of water over time.

The roadway broadened and the first building they encountered was the Lumberjack saloon.

'This'll do,' Stall said, and they turned their horses toward the hitch rail.

'Damn right it will,' Jack Murphy agreed, eyes on the building next to the saloon.

Stall and Kansas shifted their gaze to the neighbouring two-storey building. The second-storey veranda ran the width of the building and had a magnificent hand-tooled balustrade. The sign at the top of the building, painted in bold pink letters, read Silk Purse.

'Looks as though we've found a bed for the night,' the outlaw boss surmised. 'Let's get a drink and then we'll check it out.'

CHAPTER 10

Sheriff Tobias Bennett, at forty-eight, was getting on in years for his chosen profession. Despite his tired eyes and greying hair he considered himself capable of performing his duties well enough to remain in the job.

He was tall, but his stance these days tended to be more round than straight up and down. His preferred choice of apparel was brown corduroy pants and a denim coat.

About his broadening hips he wore a Colt .45 and his gunbelt bore the marks of having been let out a couple of notches.

Though small by most standards, the jailhouse comprised a big room with two cells at the back, these latter having floor-to-ceiling iron bars. Wanted posters lined the walls. A pot-belly stove stood in the corner, with a coffee pot simmering away on top.

He leaned back in his battered timber chair,

tucked his hands behind his head, then lifted his feet and placed them, boots and all, on the scarred desktop. He looked out through the jail's front window and espied a familiar face hurrying across the main street. The expression on that face was worried.

With a sigh of frustration Bennett swung his feet back to the floor and waited for the front door to crash open. When it did a middle-aged man with a red face and a receding hairline rushed in.

Thaddeus Marlow was Miller's Crossing's mayor. He was a short man, getting on in years and always wore a suit with a bow tie.

'What is it now, Marlow?' Bennett asked, resigned to the fact that demands were about to be made, but hoping that Marlow wasn't about to have him out on some fool's errand.

'You got trouble, Tobias,' Marlow gasped out. 'Big trouble.'

'Why is that?'

'You'll never guess who I just saw ride into town.'

'*Let* me guess,' Bennett said coolly. 'Wyatt Earp?'

'Red Mike Stall,' the mayor blurted out.

The sheriff sat forward in his chair. He hoped that Marlow was mistaken but he could tell from the mix of fear and anxiety on the man's face that he was telling it straight.

'Was he alone?' Bennett asked hopefully. The mayor shook his head.

'No. He had two others with him.'

'Where did they go?'

'They went over the bridge,' Marlow told him. 'I think they went into the Lumberjack.'

Bennett stood up and wandered over to the window. He stared out through the grime-covered glass at the main street. He watched the townsfolk as they went about their business, oblivious to the danger in their midst. His mind was far away, trying to work out why Stall was in Miller's Crossing.

'The bank,' he said aloud.

'What?'

'Go over to the bank, Marlow, and tell Nelson to close early today,' Bennett ordered.

'Do you think that's why they're here? To rob the bank?' Marlow asked, horrified at the thought.

'Let's hope not.'

'What are you going to do about it?' Marlow asked impatiently. 'You're paid to uphold the law. You need to get rid of them.'

'Are you goin' to back me, Marlow?'

The mayor's mouth opened and closed like that of a fish gasping for air.

'I didn't think so,' Bennett sighed, disappointment clear in his voice. Over the years they'd all offered him help when he didn't need it. Now, when he needed it, he guessed they would all be like Marlow.

Still, it was his job to protect the town and he knew that once he walked out through the door the odds were that he'd never return.

'Go on, Marlow,' Bennett urged. 'Go and get Nelson to shut the bank.'

The anxiety in the mayor's face vanished and he couldn't hide his relief at the sheriff's words.

'Yes, I'll go right now.'

After the mayor's departure Bennett walked over to the wall-mounted gun rack. He found what he wanted and took it down. It was a 12-gauge Remington coach gun with 18-inch twin barrels.

He carried it to his desk, broke it in half, opened a desk drawer and took out a couple of shells. Two only. He knew that he wouldn't need any more. Once things kicked off there wouldn't be time to reload.

Bennett slid the shells into the twin barrels, then snapped the gun closed.

He checked the loads in his Colt and slid the six-gun back into its holster; then he scooped the shotgun up from his desk and headed out through the door.

He paused on the uneven boardwalk, turned and looked back at the jail, then down at the shotgun he held. Stay or run?

He stepped down into the dusty street, knowing what he would do.

Stall and Kansas sat at a round, scarred-top table of the Lumberjack saloon and faced the front door while they worked on a bottle of red-eye. Any trouble was expected to come from that direction.

But it didn't.

The main bar-room was small but packed with tables, which left little room for anything else. It was a double-storey affair but it was narrow and longer from front to back than side to side. A small landing at the top of the stairs led on to a long hallway that ran straight back, five rooms on each side.

The interior was dim, kerosene lamps attached to the panelled walls providing minimal orange light.

The bar ran almost the room's full width, and was topped with a polished counter. A foot rail ran along the bottom.

Beneath the stairs was a hallway leading to the back entrance. From this darkened passage came Bennett, toting his cut-down coach gun.

Stall and Kansas weren't aware of his presence until they heard the twin hammers being thumbed back.

'Don't move,' said a low voice. 'If you so much as twitch, Stall, I'm goin' to paint the walls with your brains.'

'Well then,' Stall said cautiously, 'remind me not to get an itch.'

'You fellers get your hands up,' Bennett ordered.

Slowly the two outlaws raised their hands to shoulder level. The Miller's Crossing sheriff circled around until he stood and faced them. The aim of the coach gun's twin barrels never wavered from Stall's head.

'OK, now unbuckle your guns and stand up, one at a time,' Bennett said in a raised voice. He shoved the shotgun at Stall. 'You first.'

'You're a dead man, Sheriff,' Stall sneered.

'Do it, Stall. Don't give me an excuse,' Bennett cautioned. ' 'Cause right now I'm wonderin' why I don't shoot you instead and be done with it.'

Stall did as the Miller's Crossing sheriff ordered and stood there, a cold, menacing look on his face.

'Now step away from the chair,' Bennett told him.

The outlaw stepped away a couple of paces. Bennett turned to Kansas.

'Now you.'

Kansas did the same as Stall, which caused an obvious release of tension in the sheriff. Once Bennett became more aware of his surroundings he saw that every eye in the room was centred on him. He called across to Henry Stillwell, the barkeep.

'Henry, come on out here and get these guns while I take these fellers in.'

Stillwell never moved.

'Come on, Henry, get out here,' Bennett snapped impatiently.

But the barkeep remained transfixed behind the bar. That was when Bennett noticed the almost imperceptible look of fear on his face.

The sheriff frowned. *Why?*

The dry triple-click of a gun hammer being drawn back and the cold, hard gun barrel at the back of his neck made Bennett freeze.

'I guess he figures you're outnumbered, Sheriff,' said a dry, raspy voice.

In that one instant Bennett knew he was a dead man. His shoulders slumped and the coach gun's twin barrels tilted so that they pointed at the floor.

'Well now, Sheriff,' Stall's cold smile split his face, 'seems to me the boot is on the other foot. So how about you drop the scattergun. Now!'

The noise of the gun hitting the floor boards was thunderous in the heavy silence and Bennett flinched at the sound.

'What are we goin' to do with him, Mike?' Kansas asked.

'We're goin' to hang him.'

CHAPTER 11

A light breeze swept down from the snowline high above. It chilled the two riders as they sat on their horses the following morning, studying the town before them.

A large plume of dark smoke billowed up to stain the sky a dirty saddle-brown directly above Miller's Crossing.

'That can't be a good sign,' observed King.

Brolin took off his hat, ran his hand through his hair, then placed the hat back on his head. He watched in silence as the smoke continued to rise unabated.

They had moved off the trail to a rocky rise to gain a better vantage point observing what was happening in the town. As they watched from the shade of a large fir tree they saw a flicker of movement on the edge of town.

Brolin saw a horse-drawn buggy emerge from

between the buildings on the main trail. It was followed by a two-horse team hauling a buckboard, which was loaded with passengers and their belongings. Then another equipage appeared, exactly the same as the first. There followed a small procession of horses and riders, along with townsfolk on foot.

The faint popping of gunfire could be heard in the distance and the fleeing refugees' pace quickened. Brolin kneed his horse forward.

'Come on. Let's see what's happenin'.'

Brolin waved down the buggy. A short man, dressed in a suit and bow tie, sat in the driver's seat. His eyes had a certain wild look in them, akin to that of an elk fleeing a pack of wolves. Beside him was a middle-aged woman in a light-pink dress; his wife, Brolin guessed.

'Don't go that way, stranger,' the man warned, glancing back towards the town. 'If you do, it'll be certain death that awaits you.'

'What's goin' on that's got you all so scared?' Brolin asked.

'Mike Stall,' the man replied, and risked another backward look.

'Is he in your town?'

'Yes. He . . . uh . . .' another glance, 'he murdered our sheriff. Hung him from the big ponderosa in town.'

Brolin nodded and heard King mutter something under his breath.

'But he wasn't satisfied with that,' the man continued. 'He burned the jail, which in turn set fire to the stage office and the assayer's office because they're on either side.'

'Who are you?' Brolin asked.

'My name is Marlow, Thaddeus Marlow. I'm the mayor of Miller's Crossing.'

'What did they do after they set fire to the jail?' Brolin questioned.

'They got hold of Nelson. He's the bank manager,' Marlow explained. 'Stall made him open up the bank so they could get at the money. Then they shot him and set fire to the bank.'

Brolin's expression was grim, his mouth set in a thin line. He watched as more people from the town travelled past.

'Where are they now?'

Marlow shrugged. 'Who knows? They could be anywhere in town.' Marlow paused, then looked alarmed as an idea flitted into his head. 'You're not going down there, are you?'

Brolin nodded. 'If Stall is down there, then that's where I'm goin'.'

'You're crazy,' the mayor blurted out. 'If you go down there they'll kill you.'

'Maybe,' Brolin allowed. 'But I'm sure as hell goin' to kill Stall before I die.'

The gunfighter flinched as the words passed his lips. There it was. The old Brolin, the killer, the hired gun. He'd lingered just below the surface all these years and now he was back.

Marlow stared at him, then shook his head.

'I wish you luck, stranger,' he said, doubt evident in his voice.

Marlow flicked the reins. The buggy moved back on to the trail and Marlow pushed his way into the line of other refugees.

King had noticed the shift in Brolin's personality. He cleared his throat, then asked:

'What are we goin' to do?'

Brolin stared at him, his expression hard.

'You're not comin'. I don't need your help. What needs to be done I can do by myself.'

King looked indignant. 'The hell you say! I came to get those responsible for Edgar's death and that is what I aim to do.'

Brolin's anger threatened to surface but he kept it in check. Instead of rebuking King, he reached into his jacket pocket and removed the picture. His demeanour softened and he put it back.

'OK,' he told King. 'But give me your Winchester. I'll need the extra firepower of the bullets it carries.'

Without question King took the gun from his saddle boot and rode in close to pass it to Brolin.

With a flurry of movement Brolin quickly reversed the rifle, brought the butt up in a short arc and smacked it solidly into the side of the store owner's head.

King slumped sideways from the saddle and fell

to the ground, out cold.

Brolin waved down the second buckboard as it passed. The driver, a thin man with a grey beard and tired eyes drew back on the reins and the team came to a slow stop.

'Can you take this feller and his horse with you?' Brolin asked him.

'What did you hit him fer?' the man asked. 'He ain't dangerous, is he? I ain't goin' to take him if he's some kind of killer.'

'No, he ain't a killer,' Brolin said reassuringly. 'It's just that where I'm goin' he can't come.'

The man raised an eyebrow. 'Where's that?'

'Miller's Crossing.'

'Of all the damn fool things to do . . .' the man started, unable to believe Brolin could be so stupid.

'Mister?' a woman in a grey dress spoke. 'We'll take your friend there with us. Seems to me you've done him a favour. No sense in both of you getting killed.'

Brolin nodded. 'Thank you, ma'am. I'd be obliged if you could apologize to him for me when he comes to.'

The woman nodded and watched as Brolin turned the buckskin on to the trail and rode towards town, the Winchester cradled across his lap.

The memory of it all came flooding back. How it had felt, the way he used to play things out in his mind. But most of all the calmness. The acceptance that his death could be imminent. His former profession required a man to be totally devoid of emotion. Emotion could get you killed.

As he entered the town Brolin rode slowly. His eyes carefully scanned everywhere for any threat to his safety.

The smell of wood smoke overlaid with the sickening odour of burnt flesh assailed his nostrils. He'd smelt it once before and could never forget the sweet, acrid stench that threatened to turn his stomach.

Brolin thumbed back the hammer on the Winchester and rested the butt plate on his thigh so that the barrel pointed skywards; his finger rested on the trigger.

The offensive stink made the buckskin toss its head about. The gunfighter whispered a few soothing words to settle it and the pair moved further into town.

'I wouldn't go any further if I was you, mister,' a man carrying a bundle over his shoulder advised. 'Not if you want to stay alive.'

Brolin looked the speaker up and down and turned his attention to those with him: a slim-built woman in her early thirties and two children, both girls, around eight or nine years of age.

Brolin nodded; he could understand why the man was getting out.

'Where are they?' he asked. The man shrugged.

'Who knows? After they burned the jail they robbed the bank and set fire to it. Killed the manager. That's him you can smell.'

'I heard,' Brolin acknowledged. 'I was talkin' to the mayor, feller called Marlow.'

The man winced in disgust. 'I bet he was the first one out of town. If we could've got some guns together we might have stood a chance of gettin' rid of them. But once he started spoutin' about how we all needed to get the hell out of Miller's Crossing there was no chance of it happenin'.'

The gunfighter looked at the man's family once more.

'You're doin' the right thing. Now, what about Stall and his friends? Any idea?'

'If I had to guess I'd say try the saloons. Or the Silk Purse. They've locked all the whores up over there so they can't get away.' He shook his head. 'Who knows what they have in store for them?'

'Thanks,' said Brolin grimly.

'Say, you ain't goin' after them alone, are you? Do you want some help?'

The woman placed her hand on her husband's arm, alarm visible on her face.

'Frank, no.'

'Thanks, but I'll be fine.'

The man shrugged. 'Suit yourself.'

After the family had moved on Brolin proceeded along the street and found the source of the stench that still hung thickly over the town.

The bank building had collapsed into a pile of blackened rubble. Orange flames still licked greedily at parts of wooden beams but the plume of smoke was abating.

Further along he came across the smouldering ruins of the jail and the two adjacent buildings. The steady stream of townsfolk had petered out and he figured that he must be the only living soul left. Apart from the whores and the outlaws.

Brolin saw the Big Sky saloon. He climbed down from the buckskin and left it ground hitched in the street. He walked cautiously towards the saloon and climbed the steps on to the boardwalk.

Planks creaked as they took his weight; warily he crossed to the batwings and peered over them. The saloon was empty.

Brolin turned around and stepped back into the street. He crossed to the buckskin and scooped up the reins. He walked further along the street, with the animal trailing behind.

Brolin found the sheriff swinging gently at the end of a rope looped over a low, thick branch of the tall ponderosa. His face was swollen and a mottled blue colour. His tongue protruded grotesquely between his slack lips.

The gunfighter spat in the dirt and turned away from the sight. He led the horse away from the tree, up the slight incline and on to the bridge.

CHAPTER 12

King moaned softly as he stirred from the depths of unconsciousness. He rocked back and forth with the buckboard's movement as it traversed the rough trail, bumping from one deep rut to the next.

A sudden lurch shot a jolt of pain through his throbbing head. He clutched at it in an attempt to make it stop.

'How are you feelin', mister?' a woman's soft voice asked.

King fought to open his eyes. On the third attempt managed to get the lids apart, but only fractionally.

A woman's face, framed with long black hair, swirled in front of him. King was forced to squeeze his eyes shut as he tried to make the swirling stop. He cracked them open again and was able to focus this time, without a feeling of nausea.

'Where am I?' King groaned.

'We're on the trail from Miller's Crossing,' the woman informed him.

Hurriedly King tried to sit up but his head swam once more. He slumped back.

'Take it easy mister,' the woman cautioned. 'You took a nasty whack on the head.'

'Where's Br . . .' he started but caught himself before the gunfighter's name spilled out. 'Where's the man I was with?'

'He went on into town,' the driver answered. 'He sure didn't want you along with him. Good thing if you ask me. There ain't nothin' waitin' in that town but death.'

This time when King sat up he shook his head to clear it, then demanded: 'Where's my horse?'

'It's tied to the back of the buckboard,' the woman explained.

'Stop the wagon,' King snapped.

'What?' The driver whipped his head around.

'I said stop the damned wagon!'

The driver eased to a stop. King climbed down and went to where his horse was tied. He unhitched the reins and looked back up at the driver. King still had the Colt Lightning but. . . ?

'Where's my rifle?'

'Your friend took it with him,' answered the man.

King nodded curtly, then swung stiffly up into the saddle.

'Where on earth are you goin', mister?' the

woman asked.

'Back to town,' he informed her. He turned the horse about and heeled it into a gallop, back down the trail towards Miller's Crossing. The man shook his head in bewilderment.

'Damned fool!' he muttered.

Thirty minutes of hard riding returned King to their earlier observation point above the town. This time the scene was different.

The great plume of smoke was no more; instead there was a faint brown smudge against a blue backdrop.

Gone too was the procession of townsfolk who had sought to escape the cruelty of Mike Stall.

When King heard the sound it was faint, so faint in fact that he thought his ears were playing tricks. He strained hard and was able to make out the cracking of distant gunfire. King's jaw set firm. He knew what it meant and just hoped that he wasn't too late.

'Damn it!' he cursed loudly and drew the Lightning from its holster.

Without no further thought the store owner gave his mount a savage kick and sent it cannoning towards town.

After he'd crossed the river Brolin paused. Two bodies lay in the street. Both were male, their six-guns lay in the dirt beside them. It looked as though they'd tried to make a fight of it and failed.

Their clothing indicated that they were lumbermen. No wonder they had never stood a chance against Stall.

That in itself made Brolin frown. Lumbermen were known to be a breed who spoiled for a fight. They were tough men, so why hadn't they banded together to stand against Stall and his men? Where were they now? He hadn't passed them on the way in.

He could only guess they were up in the mountains felling trees.

Brolin eased back the hammer on the Winchester. He grimaced as the dry triple click sounded loud in his ears. He let the buckskin's reins go and slowly moved forward.

Three horses stood tied to the hitch rail outside the Lumberjack saloon. Without a doubt, that would be where he'd find Stall and his men.

He hoped to have the element of surprise on his side, enabling him to take them all out, but no, alas. As they say, even the best-laid plans can come undone.

'Hey, mister!' A woman's voice broke the silence.

Brolin looked up but continued his pace. A woman leaned through a second-storey window of the Silk Purse and waved frantically to draw his attention. She was young, red-headed and dressed in a pale corset that forced her milky-white breasts to bulge upward.

'Hey mister!' she called again. 'Can you help us?'

A larger blonde woman joined the redhead at the window.

'Come on, mister,' she screeched. 'Get us out of here. Quickly!'

Brolin cursed under his breath; then suddenly, as if on cue, the Lumberjack's double batwing doors burst open and three men spilled on to the boardwalk, guns drawn.

Stall was first in line; he sighted Brolin as the gunfighter brought the Winchester around to snap a shot off from the hip.

'Son of a bitch, it's him!' the outlaw snarled. 'It's Brolin.'

The Winchester's barrel spat flame and the bullet chewed splinters from the saloon's awning upright, close to the killer's head. Stall flinched instinctively and the reflexive action threw off his aim.

The shot flew wide of its mark but close enough for Brolin to feel it pass. He lurched to his left and looked for cover. He found it on the other side of the street.

He dived behind a water-filled trough just as Kansas and Murphy opened up with their six-guns.

Their bullets hammered into the trough and gouged out wooden splinters. The wicked slivers scythed dangerously through the air above Brolin. More shots dug into the damp earth beside the trough and others burned the air above it.

The Winchester whiplashed as Brolin snapped off a shot at the exposed Murphy. The slug missed and shattered the saloon's large window behind him.

Brolin dropped back behind cover as an even more ferocious storm of lead assailed his position.

Though he was behind cover Brolin felt too exposed. If he stayed where he was the outlaws would flank him and cut him down.

Stall had been thinking along those very lines. When Brolin came back up to fire again, he caught a glimpse of Kansas moving left.

Brolin fired twice at the fast-moving outlaw but the shots only kicked up dirt at the outlaw's heels. Brolin dropped back down as more shots from Stall and Murphy came at him.

Damn it! He had to move now. He looked about from his current place of refuge and tried to figure out his best escape route. The buildings behind him were no good. They were more than likely locked, and would only serve to trap him for the outlaws. The only other viable option seemed to be the river.

About a hundred feet separated him from the embankment that fell away to the raging torrent of white water below.

Now or never.

Brolin got to his feet and launched himself on his run. He'd covered no more than a few yards when a hail of bullets forced him to retreat.

Brolin dived back behind the trough, glad to be still in one piece.

'Goin' somewhere, Brolin?' shouted Stall gleefully from across the street.

The gunfighter remained silent. He had more pressing problems than becoming engaged in a yelling match with Stall.

He looked down at the Winchester and guessed there were only a few shots left in the magazine. He'd fire them, then run before they could flank him.

Brolin took a couple of deep breaths. He was about to fire when a drumming of hoofbeats hammered out on the bridge's boards.

He swung his head and saw, of all people, King, riding hell for leather towards him and waving his double-action Lightning.

As the horse thundered off the bridge King started to fire wildly. No shots found a mark, but they had the desired effect of keeping the outlaws' heads down.

'Damn fool!' Brolin cursed loudly.

The gunfighter took advantage of the cover-fire distraction and ran full tilt towards the river.

Keeping his head down, pumping his legs furiously, it still took Brolin what seemed to him like an eternity to cover the open ground.

Meanwhile, gunfire still echoed from the false-fronts that lined the street.

The drop-off loomed large in front of him when the sudden high-pitched shriek of King's horse brought him to a sliding stop. A mixture of anger and helplessness flooded through Brolin as he saw the bay down on its side and King struggling to free his trapped leg. The Colt Lightning had spilled from his grasp and now lay out of reach, leaving him vulnerable.

Through his struggles, he looked towards Brolin and their eyes met. The store owner ceased his fight to free himself.

'Go!' he screamed. 'Get away.'

Brolin paused, then took a tentative step towards the trapped King. The outlaws turned their attention back to Brolin and opened fire.

A bullet clipped his coat; another gouged a bloody furrow in his left shoulder, knocking him off balance. Down on one knee, he glanced again at King.

'Go!' King yelled again.

Another slug snapped close to Brolin's head and his survival instinct kicked in. He pushed his concerns about King aside and lunged backward over the steep embankment. He hit the slope and slid down into the Standish River's raging waters.

The moment he splashed into the fast-flowing river a bone-chilling coldness took his breath away as though he had been punched in the stomach.

Brolin opened his mouth and gasped for air. Instead, freezing mud-filled water flooded his throat and caused him choke and splutter. He fought hard to keep his head above the turbulent torrent but the strong undercurrent dragged him down.

The powerful flow carried Brolin swiftly along the rock-strewn watercourse. He let the Winchester go so that he could put all of his strength into surviving this ancient battle of man versus nature's fury.

His lungs burned in their quest for air as he was sucked below the surface once more. He intensified his efforts, hands fighting the water as he reached out and pulled back in an attempt at a crawl.

Just when Brolin thought he was winning fate dealt a hefty blow in the form of a large lump of granite.

A boulder sat proudly above the surface, powerful currents eddying about it. It was an immovable object, battered and worn down over thousands of years.

Brolin was hurled brutally against it. His head connected solidly and stars flashed before his eyes. Stunned, he lost all of the fight he'd displayed earlier. Now he was helpless; the unforgiving current sucked him below the foaming white water and out of sight.

CHAPTER 13

King watched as the gunfighter disappeared over the river's embankment. Despite his own dire predicament, a sense of relief flooded through him at the thought that Brolin was getting away.

The gunfire died away but the sound of approaching footfalls changed King's relief to fear. He renewed his struggle to free his trapped leg. It was a vain attempt; it was pinned fast beneath the dead horse.

'Murphy, check the river,' King heard Stall order.

Murphy loped across to the riverbank, leaving Stall and Kansas to tend to the trapped store owner.

'I know him,' Kansas said, recognizing King's features. 'He was on the train too. How in hell did you fellers get out of the church?'

King stayed silent.

Stall stared hard at the store owner, trying to place him. Then he nodded.

'Sure, you're the feller with the woman and the two brats.'

King bridled.

'One,' he grated through clenched teeth. 'One child. You animals murdered my boy.'

Stall shrugged nonchalantly.

'Too bad.'

Something akin to a primeval growl escaped King's lips and he renewed his struggles to be free. Never had he wanted to kill someone as much as he did right at this moment. As he fought to escape he prayed earnestly for God's help to finish this one last thing.

Murphy came running back.

'No sign,' he panted. 'He's either dead or the river took him. Either way I'd say he's dead.'

'In case you hadn't noticed,' Stall reminded him caustically, 'Brolin has a habit of comin' back from the dead.'

Murphy shrugged. 'I say he's dead.'

'And I say don't be so sure.'

'This feller won't be comin' back,' Kansas said. He cocked his six-gun and pointed it at King's head.

The store owner froze as he stared down the gaping barrel of the outlaw's nickel-plated Colt. A new surge of fear coursed through him as he waited for death to come.

Stall threw a hand out to stay Kansas's trigger finger.

'No, wait!' he snapped. 'Keep him alive for now. If Brolin is still alive he'll be back for him.'

Kansas stared hard at the outlaw boss.

'You mean we're stayin'?' His tone was one of disbelief. 'You can't be serious, Mike. We need to get gone from here. The law could show up here at any time.'

'We're stayin',' Stall insisted.

'Hell, Mike!' Murphy put in. 'After what happened with the train and what we did to the posse that was tailin' us, we can forget lawmen. These mountains are goin' to be crawlin' with soldiers. And in case you ain't noticed, there's only the three of us now. We need to leave. I for one ain't hangin' around here waitin' for a cavalry troop to come ridin' in.'

With a fluid movement Stall drew his right-side Colt and aimed it at Murphy's face.

'I said we stay.' His growl was low, menacing. 'If Brolin's alive he'll be back. I'm not leavin' here to have him on our back trail. And that's what will happen if he's alive. No, it ends here.'

Murphy stared nervously at the six-gun and swallowed the lump of fear in his throat. Then he nodded his acceptance. Stall holstered his gun and stabbed a finger at King.

'Now get him out from under that horse and into the saloon. I want to ask him some questions.'

Kansas and Murphy took King's arms and roughly wrenched him from beneath the dead horse.

'Take it easy,' the store owner protested.

'Get up,' Kansas ordered.

King staggered to his feet and straightened up. He winced as a bolt of pain shot through his injured leg. Still, he was able to put weight on it.

'Move.' Murphy's voice was harsh and a vicious shove accompanied it as King limped towards the Lumberjack saloon.

The roar of rushing water filled Brolin's ears as he ascended from the cold depths of darkness. His head wound throbbed from its forceful impact with that damned rock. He rolled on to his back and lay there trying to gather himself.

His shoulder wound burned when he moved his arm and the bright sunlight almost blinded him when he tried to open his eyes, forcing him to shut them again.

Brolin sat up drunkenly. His head swam.

He blinked his eyes again to clear his vision. Clarity returned slowly and Brolin was eventually able to take in his surroundings.

He was lying on a flat, sand-covered bench area on the southern bank, where the river curved. He had no idea how he'd managed to drag himself from the fast-flowing torrent.

Above the bench the bank was little more than a

gentle slope, covered in a blanket of lush green grass. On the opposite bank large pines over a hundred feet tall reached up to the sky.

Brolin climbed to his feet, wobbled unsteadily, then checked for the Remington. It lay in the holster. At least he had one weapon, after losing the Winchester in the river, and the Sharps was still on the horse.

He made his way slowly up the bank. Once at the top he stopped to take a break. The pain in his head had increased with the climb and his vision became blurred once more. Brolin slumped to his knees.

He put his arms out to regain his balance but to no avail. Slowly, like a giant redwood, Brolin teetered forward beyond the point of no return as the soft green carpet of grass came up to meet him. Once again, everything went black.

When Brolin came to for the second time it was dark and he was cold. He was bone-chillingly cold, wrapped in his damp clothing. Somewhere on the mountain slopes a wolf howled, its mournful sound carried eerily on the clear night air.

Brolin shivered uncontrollably; he knew he needed to get warm or the cold would kill him. A sudden gust of wind rippled through the trees with a low whistle.

Brolin got to his feet and turned right. He staggered into the darkness and followed the river back to town. He had no idea of the distance he'd been swept, but the need to get warm overrode all else and Miller's Crossing was the only place he'd find a means to do it.

Candy dabbed at the cuts and bruises on Letty's face with a wet rag, trying to clean up the dried blood as best she could.

No matter how gentle she attempted to be, every now and then the semi-conscious whore would moan in protest at the pain. Each time she did, Candy winced and apologized softly, but continued her tender ministrations.

The room they were in was on the Silk Purse's second floor, right at the front of the building.

A small kerosene lamp cast a dull orange glow throughout the meagrely furnished space. It contained a bed, an aged dresser and a small bedside table made of hardwood. A pitcher of water stood beside a shallow floral dish meant for washing in, which Candy had half-filled so that she could wet the rag she was using on Letty.

A long strand of red hair fell across her pale face as she leaned forward to clean a smear of blood from the corner of Letty's bruised mouth.

From the corners of her powder-blue eyes slid tears; they rolled down her cheek and splashed on to her unconscious friend. Stall had beaten Letty mercilessly after the plump whore had given him lip. What concerned Candy most was that she might not pull through.

The rattle of a key in the door lock drew Candy's attention. The door burst open and a man was shoved roughly inside. He fell to the floor and lay there.

'Got some company for you,' Murphy sneered.

The door slammed shut. King dragged himself to a sitting position and rubbed at his leg. One of his eyes was nearly closed and blood trickled from his nose and split lip.

'Are you OK, mister?' Candy asked in a husky voice, showing concern.

King looked across at the redhead, wiped his mouth with the back of his hand and noticed that it came away red with blood. He fingered his split lip and winced.

'I'll be fine,' he told Candy. He nodded at Letty. 'How about your friend?'

Candy's face took on a sombre expression and she shook her head.

'I don't know. She needs a doctor.'

'What happened to her?'

'That son of a bitch Stall beat her,' Candy said harshly.

King remained silent.

'I'm Candy,' she said introducing herself. 'My friend in the bed is Letty.'

King told her his name. 'How many others are there?' he asked.

'There's six more working girls,' she told him. 'All locked up in other rooms.' Candy paused for a moment, then her eyes grew wide and she leaped to her feet.

'Your friend. Did he get away?'

The store owner shrugged. 'I don't know. He went into the river.'

Candy was wearing an emerald-green dress the hem of which, King noticed now that she was standing, fell almost to the floor. The bodice stopped at her ample breasts, barely covering them. Her shoulders were pale, almost luminescent in the lamplight.

'Will he help?' she asked. 'If he's still alive, will he come back to help?'

King didn't hesitate in his answer.

'If he's alive he'll be back. You can count on it.'

CHAPTER 14

Brolin shook uncontrollably as the dark night grew bitterly cold. Snow had begun to fall and a white powder dusted his trembling shoulders. He'd staggered back towards town for the best part of two hours and was about done in.

He knew that it couldn't be much further to town and, despite his bone-weary fatigue, he knew he couldn't stop. If he did so he would die.

From the darkness loomed the buildings of Miller's Crossing; large, square, unnatural shapes that almost seemed darker than the night itself.

Further away shone a light in a window. It guided him like a moth to a flame, into the town.

Simon Ford had refused to be driven from the town that had been his home for the past five years. Partly because he'd become stubborn with age, mostly because he was the local doctor and had a critically injured lumberjack in the other room. A logging accident had brought the man in two days before and he'd still not awakened from the depths of unconsciousness.

Ford was a man in his sixties with wavy grey hair and droopy eyes. He had begun to stoop with age but his mind was as sharp as ever.

He turned another page in the leather-bound medical journal he was reading about head trauma. The living room of his small house-cum-surgery was well lit by two lamps. One stood on the mantelshelf to the left of a log fire, the other on a dark hardwood sideboard. A tall bookshelf, filled with numerous books, stood against the same wall as the sideboard.

Ford paused and looked up from his reading. He frowned and the lines on his face knitted together as he listened again for what had caught his attention. He waited a little longer. When nothing happened he shook his head and went back to his book.

The noise that had made Ford pause reached his ears again. This time it was louder, unmistakable. It came from his back door.

Ford placed the journal down on the small round-topped table beside his chair and rose to investigate.

He walked steadily to his back door, then paused to listen. The knock came again, weaker this time.

Ford reached out and grasped the doorknob. He swallowed the nervous lump in his throat and opened the door.

The man who stood before him shivered uncontrollably from the cold. Snowflakes had settled on his shoulders and his face had a tinge of blue about it.

He smiled wanly at Ford and, barely able to speak said, 'Evenin'.'

Then he fell at the doctor's feet.

The sound from the semi-darkened saloon was thunderous. Mike Stall's snores could be compared to the sound of a herd of buffalo stampeding along the street. The vibrations almost made the saloon shake.

He sat in a chair with his booted feet up on another. He was relaxed from the now two-thirds-empty bottle containing the remains of the red-eye he'd consumed.

'What are we goin' to do?' Murphy whispered to Kansas, worry evident in his voice.

'What do you mean?'

'You know what the hell I mean, Kansas!' Murphy shrilled loudly before he caught himself. He leaned in close. 'Mike's gone crazy. The only thing that hangin' around here is goin' to do is get us an invitation to a neck-tie party. How long do you think it'll be before a posse or the cavalry come ridin' into town? One night here was fine, but we shoulda rode out of here today. And all because of one man. Hell, he's goin' to get us killed!'

Kansas fingered another bottle of whiskey and nodded in agreement.

'Maybe, but he's the boss.'

The disgruntled outlaw threw back his shot and screwed his face up at the harsh liquor's slow burn. He cleared his throat and cursed.

'Hell, you're as crazy as him!'

'Maybe, but what else did you expect me to say?' Kansas nodded at Stall.

Murphy turned; his eyes widenened a fraction. Stall was no longer asleep. He was sitting there with one of his six-guns drawn and pointing at Murphy.

'Are you goin' to shut up?' His tone was menacing. 'Or am I goin' to have to shoot you to shut you up?'

Murphy dropped his gaze and turned back around. He grabbed the whiskey bottle and poured himself another shot.

'I thought so,' Stall sneered. The outlaw boss stood up.

'Where are you goin'?' Kansas asked.

Stall grabbed the bottle of red-eye from the table.

'I'm goin' next door,' he snapped, 'where I can get me a bed and some peace and quiet.'

A low keening filled the small room and steadily grew into a wail. The noise dragged King from a deep, dreamless sleep. He sat up and blinked furiously to clear his vision. Instinctively, he clutched at the empty holster before he remembered where he was.

Once his vision had cleared he glanced at Candy. The whore had a look of utter devastation on her face.

'She's dead,' Candy whimpered. 'Letty's dead.'

Her shoulders trembled then slumped as her grief at the loss of her friend overwhelmed her. King got to his feet. His body protested fiercely at the movement. He crossed the room and gently put his arms around Candy. She melted against him and buried her face into his chest. Her sobs came freely as King held her tight and tried to ease her pain.

They stood like that for several minutes before Candy pulled back. She wiped at the wet patch on his jacket with her hand.

'I'm sorry,' she apologized.

King gave her a sympathetic look. Then his expression changed and his jaw set firm. He took her arm.

'Come on, we're gettin' out of here.'

Candy wiped at her eyes, confused.

'What? How?'

'Out the side window,' King informed her.

'But it's too high!'

King ignored her protests. 'Grab a blanket. It's goin' to be cold out and you'll need it.'

Candy gently removed the blanket from the bed where Letty lay. She looked down at her friend and whispered:

'I'm so sorry, Letty.'

While Candy retrieved the blanket, King limped across to the window and opened it. A freezing gust of wind blew in, bringing with it small snowflakes. He shivered as the cold blast of air filled the room.

He stuck his head out of the window. The exposure to the cold breeze made the bare skin of his face hurt, as though it were being pricked with sharp needles. He looked down into the alley below. The window was high, but a leap was not impossible. Candy appeared beside him.

'Give me the blanket,' he said.

'What for?' she asked. King had told her she'd need it and now he wanted to take it from her.

'I'm goin' to use it to lower you part-way down,' he explained.

'But it's not long enough,' she pointed out.

'Once you get down as far as you can, you'll have to let go and drop to the alley.'

Candy was horrified.

'I can't do it, I'll still be too high.'

'You'll be fine,' King reassured her. 'Now climb out.'

With few further protests and a lot of effort, King managed to help Candy out and start lowering her down. When they ran out of blanket she was still fifteen feet from the ground.

'OK, let go,' King told her.

'I . . . can't,' Candy stammered.

'You must.'

'No, I can't.'

Before King could say more he heard the sound of heavy footsteps coming along the hall. They stopped outside his room and he heard the key rattle in the door lock.

He glanced at the door, then back to Candy, who was clinging to the blanket as if her life depended upon it.

'Sorry,' King murmured. He let the blanket go.

When Candy realized she was falling her scream pierced the night. It stopped abruptly when her rump hit the snow-covered ground.

'What the hell?'

King whirled and saw Mike Stall standing in the doorway, a Colt in his fist. The outlaw snapped a shot off and splinters flew from the window frame near King's head. He ducked instinctively and watched with horror as Stall took deliberate aim.

King had no time to think. To pause was to die. He did what was needed to survive and threw himself out of the window.

The second shot crashed in the small room and glass from the window shattered because the store owner was no longer there.

King fell like a stone. When he landed he felt as though he'd been run under in a stampede. The air whooshed from his lungs and pain shot through every part of his body.

In the distance he could hear Candy's screams;

as his head began to clear the screams grew louder.

King lurched as though drunkenly to his feet. He looked about, saw her, clutched her slim arm and started to drag her down the alley away from the street.

Stall leaned out of the window and fired two more shots at the fleeing couple. Then, round the corner of the building, guns drawn, came Kansas and Murphy.

'What's goin' on?' Kansas called out to his boss.

'The woman and the damned greenhorn have escaped,' Stall bellowed. 'Get the hell after 'em!'

'In case you hadn't noticed, it's damn well snowin',' Kansas pointed out. 'And you want us to go traipsin' about in it to bring back a girl and a greenhorn?'

'I don't care about the girl,' Stall roared even louder, making a point. 'But I do want that feller back *pronto*.'

Stall disappeared back inside the room and slammed the window.

'I told you he was damned crazy,' Murphy grumbled.

'Just shut up and help me look,' Kansas snapped.

They hunted for the escapees for an hour before the bitter cold drove them back indoors. When they entered the saloon, covered in wet snow, they found Stall waiting.

'Well?' he demanded.

Kansas shrugged and sat down at the table where he and Murphy had been drinking. He popped the cork from the bottle and took a long swig.

'There ain't no sign of 'em,' he gasped as the alcohol burned his throat. 'We looked around but couldn't see hide nor hair of 'em anywhere.'

'Well, get the hell out there and keep lookin',' the outlaw leader ordered. Kansas shook his head.

'Not like this, Mike.'

Stall leaned forward, his eyes turned to slits.

'What do you mean?'

Murphy backed away from the pair. The look on Stall's face was one he'd seen before.

'If we go back out there now we'll die. The cold will kill us sure as shootin',' Kansas explained. 'The longer we stay out there, the wetter we'll become and then we'll freeze to death.'

Stall mulled it over for a short time, then he nodded.

'Fine. But you're both goin' back out there when the sun comes up. And that's final.'

King and Candy managed to get over the river without being seen. From there they kept to the shadows until King stopped.

'We need to get inside or we'll die out here.'

Candy shivered uncontrollably. The blanket meant to keep her warm lay back on the ground in the alley.

King knocked on the door of the first house they came to. When no one answered he tried the knob. It was locked.

'Do you know who lives here?' he asked Candy.

'The mayor.'

King nodded, clenched his jaw and drew back his leg. He gave the door a savage kick. With a loud crack the timber around the latch splintered and the door flew open.

They walked inside. King closed the door and propped it shut with a chair. Inside the house was almost as cold as it was outside. Candy stood shivering in the darkness.

'Let's find the bedroom,' King said. 'We need to get you warm.'

They checked the rooms until they found the one they wanted. Candy took off her dress and climbed into bed in her undergarments. King climbed in beside her.

'Thank you, for what you did for me,' Candy said softly. 'For getting me out of there, I mean.'

King could feel her body still trembling beside him so he moved in close to her and reached out.

'What are you doing?' she asked, drawing back from him.

'I'm just tryin' to help you get warm is all,' King explained. 'Body heat from another person is the quickest way to warm you up.'

'Oh.'

They snuggled in close and King tried to make

light their situation to help Candy feel more at ease.

'I'm sure glad my wife ain't here,' he said. Then he added, 'Once the sun comes up we'll see if we can find some help.'

He realized then that the soft, supple body he was holding had stopped shivering. The sound of exhausted snores filled the darkness.

CHAPTER 15

The snow fell all night across Miller's Crossing. On the following morning dawn's watery light revealed a thick white powdery blanket draped over the whole town. The sky was overcast and bleak, the air frigid and biting.

Inside the home of Doctor Simon Ford the log fire kept the outside chill at bay and the rooms inside at a constant temperature.

Brolin stirred, then came awake with a start. He felt the pressure of a hand on his shoulder and a man's voice saying: 'Take it easy, Mr Brolin. You're safe here.'

First, Brolin realized that he was lying in a bed and second, the man had used his name. As the doctor's face swam into focus, Brolin asked: 'How do you know my name?'

'You talk a lot in your sleep.'

Brolin closed his eyes and sighed. 'Where am I?'

'You're in Miller's Crossing,' Ford informed

him. 'I'm Simon Ford, the doctor. This is my house.'

Brolin sat up and looked about the room. Other than the bed, there was a drawer cabinet, a night stand and a wash table with a dish and a pitcher for water. In the far corner stood a wooden dining chair, just to the left of a window. The door was open and he could feel the warmth drifting in.

'Where's my gun?' he asked Ford.

'I've hung it over a chair in the kitchen.'

Brolin frowned and looked at the doctor. 'Why are you still in town? I thought everybody had upped and quit.'

'This is my home. Nobody has the right to scare me from it,' Ford replied firmly. 'Besides, I have a man in the other room who has a head injury and hasn't woken up yet.'

Brolin swung his legs over the side of the timber-framed bed and rested his feet on the carpeted floor.

'Where do you think you're going?' Ford asked.

'I got me some men to kill, Doc,' Brolin told him.

'Stall?'

'Yeah. That's right.' Brolin went on to fill Ford in on the previous day's events.

When he'd finished, the doctor said: 'From what I've heard about you, Mr Brolin, and what you've just told me, it is hard to picture you as the cold-blooded killer the stories declare you are.'

'Don't let what I've told you fool you, Doc,' Brolin told him. 'I've done my share of killin'. Some of it questionable. But what they said I did to the trail crew was lies. That was Stall. Now I figure it's time for payback.'

Ford was about to say something when there came a loud, urgent knock at his door. He looked puzzled. He was thinking along the same lines as Brolin: that most, if not all of the town's citizens had fled when things became wild.

'Get me my gun,' Brolin ordered.

While the doctor was gone Brolin found his clothes laid over a chair in the corner. When he put his shirt on his wounded shoulder felt a little stiff, but the doctor had cleaned it and bandaged it.

The knocking continued.

When Ford returned, Brolin was mostly dressed. He took the Remington from the doctor and buckled it on.

'Right,' said Ford, 'let's see who it is.'

When Ford opened the front door, Brolin stood behind it with his six-gun cocked. He waited and listened.

'Doctor Ford, we saw your smoke. May we come in?' a woman's voice pleaded.

More than one person, Brolin thought.

'Well. . . .' Ford hesitated a moment, 'I guess. But who's your friend?'

One other person. Brolin tensed. He guessed it

was the doctor's way of letting him know the other person was a stranger.

'He helped me get away from those men,' the woman explained. 'His name is Emmett.'

Brolin stepped round the open door and looked at the two people standing in the doorway.

'Let 'em in, Doc,' Brolin told Ford. 'King's one of the good guys.'

The pair walked through the door and they all went on through to the living room. King stared at Brolin, barely able to contain his relief that the gunfighter was there in the same room.

'Damn it! You're alive.'

'So it would seem,' Brolin answered. 'What happened to you?'

'We escaped from them last night,' King answered. He related to the gunfighter the events of his ordeal after Brolin had gone into the river.

When he'd finished Ford disappeared; he soon returned with four mugs of steaming hot coffee. He left again and came back with a dress for Candy. He held it out for her.

'Please wear it. It was my late wife's. I'm sure she wouldn't mind.'

Candy hesitated.

'Please; it will be warmer than the one you have,' Ford urged her, smiling reassuringly.

Candy took it. 'Thank you.'

'You can change through there.' Ford pointed

at a closed door. After she was gone King turned to Brolin.

'What are we goin' to do?' he asked.

'*We* are goin' to do nothin',' Brolin told him. '*I*, on the other hand, am goin' out there to put an end to this.'

'Not without me you ain't,' King protested.

'We've been through this before,' Brolin said impatiently. 'You ain't comin'. This is what I do – did. Besides, this is between me and Stall.'

'They killed my son.' King seethed. 'If you think you can stop me, you go right ahead and try.'

Brolin knew the store owner wasn't going to change his mind. He could see it in his face. His eyes blazed, his jaw was set firm. Brolin nodded.

'OK. You do what I say, when I say it.'

'Fair enough.'

'And no questioning when I tell you what to do. If I tell you to do something, it's for a reason. More than likely keep you from gettin' killed.' Brolin turned towards Ford. 'Is there a place in town where we can get some more guns? A gunsmith maybe?'

Ford nodded. 'There's a gunsmith's shop down the street a little way.'

Brolin thanked Ford, found his boots and finished getting dressed. He moved to leave, then turned to King.

'Come on then,' he said, 'let's go and find you somethin' to shoot with.'

Outside the snow had stopped falling, leaving everything covered in a crisp blanket of white. The two men found the gunsmith's shop situated beside the blacksmith's.

Brolin hammered on the door with a fist. When no one answered he broke the lock and they went inside.

The interior was small and dim. Brolin looked about, trying to find something to suit. Along the back wall was a timber gun rack filled with rifles and shotguns. In front of it was a display cabinet where the six-guns were kept.

Brolin walked over to the gun rack first and selected a sawed-off shotgun. He passed it to King.

'Take this,' he ordered. 'It'll only fire two shots but it'll give you more chance of hittin' somethin'.'

He left the rifles where they were. If things went the way he expected the range would be close and they wouldn't need them.

Next, Brolin moved to the glass-topped counter and looked at the handguns. Inside were a matching pair of Colt Peacemakers. He took them out and looked about the room until he found a twin-holster gunbelt. He unbuckled the Remington and passed it to King.

'Put it on,' he told him. 'After you fire them two shots from the scattergun, you may need it.'

King strapped the gunbelt on while Brolin found some boxes of cartridges for the Colts and the scattergun. He filled the loops on the new belt, then the Peacemakers. He buckled on the belt, then used the rawhide thongs to tie the guns down.

Once finished, he adjusted them so they sat comfortable. Then he relaxed. King watched Brolin, curious as to what he was doing.

Then it happened.

In a blur of movement the twin Colts seemed to leap into the gunfighter's hands already cocked. King stood there, blinking in wonderment.

Brolin slipped them back into the holsters and nodded, satisfied. He'd finally come full circle. Brolin the gunfighter was back.

'Don't tell me. They weren't anywhere to be seen.' Stall's voice dripped with sarcasm.

'That's about it,' Kansas agreed. The outlaw boss lurched to his feet.

'If you want somethin' done right, do it yourself. Come on, damn it!'

CHAPTER 16

'If we don't come back, Doc, get out of town,' Brolin directed. 'It'll be safer for you.'

'I can't leave my patient,' Ford told him.

Brolin shrugged. 'Up to you.'

The gunfighter reached into his pocket and took out the picture, thankful the river hadn't taken it from him. He gave it to Ford.

'If I get killed out there, can you to send a letter to. . . ?'

The doctor nodded. 'Sure; just tell me where.'

Ford wrote down where the letter was to go and put both it and the picture on his mantelshelf above the fireplace.

Once more, from habit, Brolin checked the loads in his Peacemakers.

'Stay inside until we get back,' he said. Then to King, 'It's time.'

After they had left Candy turned her concerned look to the doctor.

'Do you think they'll be OK?'

'I sure hope so, Candy,' Ford said quietly. 'I sure hope so.'

Brolin and King were making their way along the snow-covered main street towards the bridge when the three outlaws appeared in front of them.

Kansas stood in the centre, with Stall on his left and Murphy to his right. As they approached they fanned out across the street to make harder targets.

Brolin let his right hand rest on the butt of his six-gun.

'Is that scattergun cocked?' he asked King.

'Yes.' King sounded nervous.

'When this starts, take the feller on the left,' Brolin told him. 'Give him both barrels, throw the scattergun away, then get your six-gun working. Don't stop until they're all down.'

King swallowed hard. 'OK.'

Less than twenty yards separated the two groups when they stopped.

'I see you're still alive,' Stall observed. 'I had me a feelin' you'd be back.'

'It's time for all this to end, Stall,' Brolin said.

Stall's cold gaze settled upon King.

'Step aside, greenhorn,' he warned him. 'This is a game for men. Not some dandy such as yourself.'

'I'm stayin'.'

'As you wish.'

'When you're ready, Stall,' Brolin's words were quiet, yet sounded deafening in the tense situation.

Stall licked his lips nervously. He wiped his sweaty palms on his jacket, then settled.

'I know one thing,' he stated. 'This time, you're goin' to stay dead.'

Hands flashed and guns came out. The weapons snapped into line and it began.

If there had been witnesses they would have sworn that the leaden sky above the town had opened up as a thunderous roar from the shotgun drowned everything out.

Brolin was still as fast as he'd ever been. He squeezed the Colt's trigger and it roared into life. Kansas went down with a bullet wound in his chest.

Brolin felt the impact of a slug as it burned deep. He shifted his aim to cover Stall, but the outlaw leader had turned tail after his first shot and was running.

Brolin fired at him. The slug hit high in the right side of his back. Stall lurched forward but remained on his feet. He kept going into an alley and disappeared.

Brolin shifted his aim across to Murphy, but he needn't have worried. The shotgun had done its bloody work and the outlaw was a pile of bloodstained rags in the snow.

'Are you OK?' Brolin asked King.

The store owner was stunned at the violence of

what had just happened.

'Yeah, I . . . think so,' he stammered. 'I'm wounded, though. My shoulder.'

He pulled back his shirt to reveal the red mark where a bullet had torn a furrow in his flesh.

'You ain't the only one,' Brolin said, feeling his own wound start to burn.

He didn't have to look to know that he'd been hit hard. He was still on his feet and that was what mattered.

He started off after Stall. The blood had begun to run freely from the wound in his chest. He tried to ignore the pain, grinding his teeth together.

When he turned into the alley he found it empty. A wave of intense pain swept through him and he staggered before regaining his balance.

His pants were becoming soaked now as blood flowed freely. His vision blurred a little and he shook his head to clear the cobwebs.

The alley led in to another street, where there were occasional vacant lots between the buildings. Stall was nowhere in sight, but as he looked down the street Brolin saw a clear blood trail leading away to his right. Thank God it had snowed! he thought.

The gunfighter followed the bright-red trail. He decided that, judging from the amount of blood the outlaw was losing, he had been hit every bit as hard as he, Brolin, had.

Brolin drew level with a laundry and stopped as

another fierce wave of pain assailed his senses. He screwed his eyes shut tightly as he willed it to stop.

After it had passed he moved on. His legs were beginning to feel like lead. He was weak from blood loss and needed to find Stall soon, or he wouldn't be able to continue.

As he trudged onwards his legs got heavier with each step. Blood was still flowing from the wound in his chest.

The crack of a gunshot was quickly followed by the slam of a bullet into his midriff.

Brolin slumped down on to his knees as a weird numbness spread throughout his body. The Peacemaker had fallen from his grasp and lay beside him in the snow-covered street.

Another gunshot roared. The slug whacked into the ground beside him.

Brolin looked up to see Stall stagger out into the open. His face was a mask of hatred and pain. The outlaw boss raised his gun and fired yet again. The bullet dug into the hardpack in front of Brolin.

Stall took a lurching step forward and fired once more. The bullet passed close enough to fan Brolin's cheek.

Another painful step forward and Stall took deliberate aim. The six-gun he held in his fist waved about as he fought against its weight. His strength was ebbing fast as lifeblood drained away.

'I ain't goin' to miss this time, Brolin, you son of a bitch,' Stall snarled.

With all the willpower he could muster, Brolin drew the left-side Peacemaker and shot Stall in the chest. The impact knocked Stall back. Brolin cocked and fired again. Stall's heart stopped beating as the .45-calibre slug smashed into it, turning it to mush.

He went down on his back, his six-gun fell from his grip. His back arched, then he was still.

Brolin knelt there briefly and looked at the body of the man he'd just killed. He felt nothing. No joy, no relief, no emotion whatsoever.

The world began to spin around him. Darkness descended; then Brolin fell on to his side and lay still.

CHAPTER 17

It was sound that broke through to him first, then the swirls of light and dark. He tried to will his eyes to open but darkness claimed him once more.

The next time Brolin came to he took in his surroundings There was a lamp casting a dull orange light about his room. He closed his eyes and tried to speak. All that escaped his parched throat was a raspy moan.

He heard a woman's voice and he felt the calming touch of a soft hand.

Brolin relaxed and felt a wave of exhaustion sweep over him, and once more descended into darkness.

The next time he came to his eyes snapped open and his first thought was: I'm alive. An incoherent noise escaped his lips.

'Easy, son,' said the Miller's Crossing doctor. 'Just take it easy.'

Brolin relaxed a little and stared at the ceiling.

Bandages swathed the top half of his body. Thoughts were jumbled inside his foggy mind. One at a time they cleared and he was able to piece together what had happened.

'Stall?' he gasped out.

'Here.' Ford held a cup to his lips. 'Drink this. Not too much, mind. You don't want to overdo it.'

Brolin took a sip, coughed, then took another.

'Stall?' he questioned again, his voice clearer.

'He's dead, son,' Ford told him. 'You killed him. The others are all dead too.'

Brolin remembered the store owner.

'King?'

'He's fine. I patched him up and he's been staying at the hotel.'

Brolin frowned at the word staying. How long had he been out to it? He looked about the room; it was small and sparsely furnished, much as one might expect of a hospital room. Sounds on the street broke through his thoughts. He looked confused.

'How long. . . ?'

He was interrupted by a knock on the room door.

Ford opened it slightly and murmured something to the person on the other side. He turned back to the gunfighter.

'Do you feel up to a visitor?'

'Sure. Send him in,' Brolin said, expecting it to be King.

To his surprise it wasn't King. The person who entered was a woman. Tall, slender, with long black hair and hazel eyes. Her face was fine featured, almost delicate. Anyone not acquainted with her might have put her age at thirty-five. The surprise on Brolin's face was immediate.

'Anna!'

His wife moved in close and kissed him tenderly on the cheek.

'I'm so happy you're awake, Matt.' She smiled. A broad smile, showing even white teeth. 'You had us worried.'

'I'll leave you to it,' Ford said. He left the room.

'What are you doing here?' Brolin asked.

'The doctor sent word saying you'd been shot,' Anna explained. 'Don't be mad. We had to come. They said you could die. As it is, you've been unconscious for the best part of two weeks. With infection and temperatures, it was touch and go for a long time.'

Brolin raised his eyebrows.

'We? You mean Clara is here with you?'

His wife nodded. 'Yes. She is with Candy.'

'You left her with a. . . ?'

'Matt Brolin, you watch your mouth,' Anna warned sternly.

Another knock sounded and King poked his head through the cracked door.

'Can I come in?'

Anna smiled warmly. 'Of course you can,

Emmett. You're more than welcome.'

King stepped into the room and smiled at Brolin, more with relief than happiness.

'The doc says you're goin' to live.'

'I feel like I've been run over by a herd of buffalo.'

King smiled again, but then a look of concern quickly descended like a dark cloud across his face. It seemed as though he had something to say but couldn't find the right words to say it.

'Out with it, Emmett,' Brolin prompted him.

'Huh, out with what?'

'You know. I can tell there's somethin' wrong.'

'I'm sorry, Brolin, but the new sheriff and the town judge are on their way over here to see you,' King explained. 'There's been talk of a trial and all.'

'Oh, Matt!' Anna gasped. 'What will we do?'

Before Brolin could respond there came another knock on the door and three men filed into the room with Dr Ford. Brolin recognized one of the three as the mayor of Miller's Crossing, but the other two were strangers.

'Somethin' I can do for you gents?' Brolin asked.

King slipped into a corner and waited to see what would happen. Anna, on the other hand, stood proudly beside her husband.

It was the mayor who spoke first.

'Mr Brolin, we would like to thank you for what you did for Miller's Crossing.'

'We?'

Marlow nodded. 'Yes. Myself, Sheriff Wayne and Judge Burns.'

Brolin looked the other two men over. Wayne was a big man with an air of confidence about him. Something he'd need if he was to make it as a lawman. Burns, though, was short and thin.

'I take it this isn't a social visit,' Brolin remarked. 'Not when you've got the infamous gunfighter and killer Brolin in your midst.'

Marlow remained silent and left it up to Burns to speak.

'Brolin,' the judge started, 'the sheriff is here to arrest you.'

'Oh no!' Anna gasped, and her hand flew to her mouth.

'Hell, Judge,' King burst out loudly. 'After all he's done for this town, for the people on the train? You want to arrest him for somethin' that happened ten years ago – that he had nothin' to do with? It ain't right.'

Brolin held up his hand to quieten the store owner.

'Hold up, Emmett. I was there. I'm not disputin' the fact.'

'But Matt . . . Anna started.

Brolin looked at the hurt in his wife's eyes.

'We always knew this could happen,' he reminded her softly.

The judge cleared his throat.

'Now before you all get carried away, we'd best sort out a few things.'

'What's there to sort out?' Anna snapped; her eyes sparkled with tears, but beneath the moisture they blazed with anger. 'You are arresting my husband for murder.'

'No, ma'am,' Burns shook his head. 'We believe your husband had nothing to do with the death of the trail crew.'

'Then why in hell are you arrestin' him?' King asked exasperatedly.

'Because, like Mr Brolin said, he was there,' Burns pointed out. 'And that makes him an accessory to a crime.'

'So what does it mean, Judge?' Brolin asked.

'My question to you is: if you were to come before me at trial, how would you plead?'

'Guilty, I guess,' Brolin answered. 'Ain't no way of gettin' around it. If I was to plead guilty, what would my sentence be?'

'Well, it would be up to the officiating judge to decide, meaning me,' Burns pointed out. 'But you see, we've had ourselves a discussion and have decided what you have done for this town cannot be ignored.'

'What do you mean?' Brolin asked warily. Burns turned to the doctor.

'How long until he would be fit enough to stand trial?'

'Ten days maybe,' Ford answered.

'That will do fine,' Burns replied. 'Mr Brolin, you've been found guilty of the crime. . . .'

'Hang on just a damned minute!' King erupted.

'Before any of you say more,' Burns raised his voice, 'let me finish. The sentence I am imposing upon you shall be ten days.'

It was Anna who broke the stunned silence. 'Does that mean. . . ?'

'Yes, ma'am, it does,' Burns confirmed. 'Your husband will serve out his sentence in this very room. And in ten days, when he is well enough to leave, he will do so a free man.'

'I don't know what to say, Judge,' Brolin managed to get out.

'Don't say anything at all, Mr Brolin, just get well and stay out of trouble.'

'I think I can manage that.' Brolin smiled. 'Thank you, Judge.

'No, Mr Brolin, it is we who thank you.'

'There's one other thing, Brolin.' The sheriff stepped forward. 'The small matter of a reward.'

Brolin looked over at King, who shook his head. He turned his gaze back to the sheriff and also shook his head.

'Give it to the town, Sheriff. We didn't do this for the money.'

'Yeah, well. . . .' Wayne let his voice trail away.

The three men filed out of the room. Once they were gone Anna launched herself at Brolin, forgetting his injuries. She kissed him long and hard as tears – now of joy – washed down her cheeks.

'You're hurting me,' Brolin managed to say.

Anna drew back, her face reflecting her shock at having forgotten herself.

'Oh Lord! Matt, I'm sorry.'

They all burst out laughing. When things had quieted some, Brolin turned his attention to King.

'How are you doin', Emmett?'

The store owner knew what Brolin was asking.

'I'm OK I guess,' he replied. 'It's all startin' to sink in now. When we were huntin' them outlaws it gave me somethin' to focus on and push the hurt to one side. But once it was over, it all came back and left a hollow feelin' down deep.'

'Yeah, it can do that,' Brolin told him. 'Have you let your wife know you're OK?'

'Yeah.' King nodded. 'I'm not lookin' forward to goin' back. Without Edgar around, things won't be the same.'

'Have you thought about a new start for your family?' Brolin asked.

King shrugged. 'I don't know. I haven't really thought much about anythin'.'

Brolin looked across at Anna, who gave him a small nod.

'I could use a partner in my store in Oregon,' Brolin said. 'If you would like to move your family out there, we could work the store and split it fifty-fifty.'

King chuckled. 'You, a store owner?'

'A man has to make a living somehow. Bills don't pay themselves,' Brolin pointed out. 'I'd be proud to have you as a partner. What do you say?'

'I'll think about it.'

Brolin smiled. 'Fair enough.'

Suddenly the door burst open and a little girl with long black tresses, similar to her mother's, ran into the room. She was no more than six years old and had sparkling brown eyes. Clara looked very much like her mother.

'Daddy!' she screamed, the biggest smile splitting her pretty face.

Clara leapt on to Brolin's bed, causing him to wince. A pair of skinny arms locked around his neck and squeezed.

Brolin held her tight and felt a great tiredness overwhelm him.

'When are we going home?' Clara asked him.

Brolin looked across at Anna who stood there smiling.

'Soon, baby girl,' he said softly. 'Very soon.'